A Sharing Of Souls

Standing on the ledge he looked over to welcome the sweet embrace of death.

He remembered hearing her whispers.

A soothing voice amongst the roars of his own self-destruction.

CHAPTER 1-

As he opened his eyes to the grey void a symphony of alarm clocks began. Standing with the balance of a hungover crane he shuffled towards the closet size bathroom. Turning the knob, the shower began its usual murderous squeak.

"Wash away this boring fucking life" he said aloud.

After his five peaceful minutes of back-and-forth water temperatures, he stepped out onto the discolored tile.

Wiping away the fog from the mirror he only saw a stranger in the reflection. Iris miller is your average run of the mill millennial. Long hair with faded sides, clothes that never match, and an arm full of tattoos that depict what makes him "unique".

Growing up in six states and over a dozen schools he never really developed acceptable social skills. Iris did have one thing that helped him navigate through life. His inability to feel.

The doctors described it as "Bipolar Depression", and after that diagnosis everything became horizontal. "Horizontal" the word he uses to describe events and life. For if things are horizontal, they can only go left or right. Good or Bad. Life and Death.

A series of directions, and after a while thinking left and right about everything becomes so dull. Contemplations of suicide and death by cop do not even cross his mind.

To cope with his lack of a soul Iris goes to the roof of his apartment complex. Up there above all the crying and youthful sex... he sits looking at the city skyline. Seeing the clouds of poison making their home in the atmosphere. Closing his eyes and listening to the sirens.

Funny how hearing such an annoying fucking noise means something important is happening. Be it life or death. Everything has become directions and sounds. Sometimes he likes to stand on the ledge. Where his toes can hover over the brick and he sways.

Sways back and forth. Forward onto the journey of death and backward into the monotonous mess of life. Left or right. Back and forth. Sound or silence.

Collecting his final thoughts, he stepped back onto the safety of the roof, and began his descent to the stairwell.

"Returning to normality" he thought.

Yet right as he was about to open the door to the jigsaw stairwell, he heard a voice.

"Hey man you mind giving me a hand?" A stranger spoke.

"With what?" Iris replied.

"I need help tying off." The stranger spoke.

"Excuse me?" Iris replied.

"I need you to put this belt around my arm and pull it tight."

"I know what tying off is, but I'm caught off guard by the question like who fucking asks that dude"?

"Well kid it's a fucked-up world we live in."

"I can't argue with that."

"So, going to help?"

"Fuck it. Why the hell not"

Iris walked towards the bold stranger to assist with his consumption.

"So how long have you been using tar?"

"I'm not a fucking dope fiend. Its stem."

"I've never heard of it. What is it?"

"It's everything. Its hope and love. yin and yang. sex and purity."

For the first time in his entire life Iris may have found the cure to his lack of feeling.

"Would you mind if I gave it a try?"

"Sure, man but brace yourself."

The clouds gave the gift of much needed shade as this new stranger began to fill the syringe with a life that Iris never knew. So many possibilities. So many emotions he had never felt. All sitting in a small plastic tube with a sharp point. Like a bumble bee with the power of god inside it's stinger.

"Take a deep breath" The stranger spoke.

Iris plunged the needle into his arm. At first, he felt nothing except the needle point. Then out of nowhere he was swept away. Everything seemed to slow down at an incredible rate. The entire city fell silent to watch as he ventured into the unknown. Iris took a breath.

Five... four... three... two... one...

His eyes rolled back into his head and the journey began. Waves of colors, sounds of laughter, and for once in his insignificant life he felt something so foreign to him. Joy.

A smile crept its way across his face, a movement his muscles had never experienced. A solitary tear rolled down his cheek.

Everything was clear for the first time in his life. He had made a best friend with a piece of himself that he never knew before. His soul.

Iris had finally found himself. He was home.

CHAPTER 2-

The light crept through the blinds making a piano key pattern of gold across their marital bed. To open his eyes to such a beautiful creature and realize that it was not a dream. No not a dream, but a moment of clarity he gets to experience every morning.

She is the pulse in his heart. The driving force that made him go on. The way her eyelids barely open when she starts to wake up. Giving just a glimpse of those beautiful autumn eyes. Eyes full of October skies and November leaves. She was his muse. He loved her with everything he had. So much that it hurt to not be close to her.

James Grayson had everything he ever could have asked for. A loving marriage with his soul mate, a beautiful little daughter named Ellie who he loved with all his heart, and a house he had built with his own hands. James had a routine.

A routine which he could never grow tired of. Every morning he awoke to the sun in his eyes. A warm reminder that he was alive.

Making his way down the mahogany stairs he had cut and shaped himself he reminisced. Each step making him feel proud and manly. The bottom step was always greeted by his chocolate Labrador Boomer. James got Boomer as a pup and they had been attached since that day.

Boomer even introduced James to the love of his life at the local park. Everything close and everything comfortable. That is the way James preferred his life. Close and comfortable. Family life was spent in seclusion.

James had always dreamed of living in a house that in its core was just a big piece of art. Glass, stone, and wood. Light and dark tones. Circles and Squares.

Walking to the end of the road to grab the paper was always a great way to start his morning. For on his way back he could stop and appreciate what he had built. To be reminded that his hard work had paid off.

His house was his expression of who he was. Tucked amongst the forest. Secluded yet open. Close and comfortable. As he picked up his newspaper and began his stroll back to the house, he heard something familiar.

An old Indian scout motorcycle came speeding out from under the tree covered road. The rider was muscular and clean cut. Every detail about him pointed towards obsessive compulsive disorder and self-centered tendencies.

James knew him as cooper. He was James's partner at work. A job they both kept quiet about due to its hand in the darker spectrum of things. Yet it was a job they both kept doing because of its seven-figure salary.

Cooper pulled up and got off the bike. The weight shift let out a noise that could only explain that he was heavier than he looks and all solid muscle. The job for which they both had required both to have an extensive fitness regimen and military history.

They always treated each other like equals, but deep-down cooper longed to surpass James in every category.

Cooper was jealous. He wanted it all. The wife, the child, and the house. The house was a painful slap in the face to him. All he had ever known was section eight housing and abusive foster parents. That is why he joined the military. To get away from it all and wipe his slate clean. Cooper envied James to the point he was willing to do whatever was necessary to be better than him.

A bitter rivalry that brewed inside and yet only one party knew it existed. James loved cooper like a little brother. Taught him everything about their line of work and welcomed him into his family with open arms.

Cooper stared at him with such a fury it felt like his tears were acid burning their way out of his eyes. "Soon enough all this will be mine" he thought while giving James a mannequin smile.

"James our next assignment is tomorrow so be ready" Cooper stated.

"Thanks for the heads-up coop" James replied.

"Yea whatever"

"Something wrong brother?"

At that point coopers' eyes were so sharp they could have been mistaken for daggers. Daggers of poison and deceit.

"Yea sorry man just didn't get much sleep." He assured James.

"Alright well rest up and I'll meet you at the harvester tomorrow."

As cooper walked away James could not help but feel like something was bothering his old friend, but he was a closed book. No use in even trying to figure out what it was.

"Hey coop one last thing. I'm proud of you."

He stopped in his tracks. A war raged inside of him. A war between love and hate. The casualties of this bitter rivalry had only just begun.

"Thanks James."

Cooper kick started his classic age bike and sped off down the dusty road. Waves of gasoline fumes and dust floated across the countryside.

James took one last appreciative look at all he had made in his life. He has everything a man could ask for. Sometimes he thought "at what cost was I given all these blessings?" for his career was one filled with sin and thievery. Only it was not some priceless piece of art or safe filled with jewels. James

Grayson was in a vampiric field of work. Stealing life from the weak.

A master of deception and death. One day he would have to pay the ultimate price for what he had done. A day that was coming a lot sooner than he ever could have imagined.

The sound of sizzling heat broke the early morning silence as James cracked three eggs into a pan. He proceeded to grinding coffee beans as the eggs cooked. He did not believe in short cuts. No bottled juice or pre ground coffee beans. Everything should be done by hand. That was his motto. You can't trust everyone, but you can trust your own hands.

His hands had produced everything he had even his own child was delivered using his own two hands. James had an advanced knowledge of almost every activity a human being can do.

So, he never trusted anyone else besides his wife to do anything for him. He made all the dinners by hand. With meat that he butchered himself. Everything close and comfortable. Tomorrow he was to leave to meet cooper at the harvester. So, tonight was to be special for him and Ellery.

She was the love of his life so he figured she deserved a night she would always remember. He sent her off to the city so she would be preoccupied as he turned their home into a den of romance. Spending hours stringing little paper lanterns through the trees and moving a small wooden table into a clearing in the woods.

It was to be perfect. Every little detail spoke words of love and affection. He had prepared a three-course meal and had a special bottle of Italian merlot from 1925 shipped over night to his house.

Seven thousand dollars for a bottle of old grapes was his opinion but he knew that she loved aged wine. As he finished preparing everything, he heard her car pull into the driveway. He cut all the lights out and waited for her.

Ellery walked towards the dark house worried something may have been wrong. Luckily, she dropped Ellie off at her grandmother's house before heading home. As she peered into the dark house through the glass on the front door, she felt her heart race. Slowly inserting the key into the lock and turning the tumblers. The door flung open, and a hand covered her mouth. Everything went dark.

She opened her eyes to see trees lit up and candles burning on a table in front of her. She heard the crickets and the forest dwellers singing their melodic tones. Setting a mood for her and the love of her life.

There he was. Walking tall and proud towards her with a bouquet of yellow lilies and a bottle of wine in the other. She had never seen such a handsome specimen in her entire life, and he was all hers. Forever.

"Hello sweetheart I sure have missed you" he said in a stern but soft voice.

"Hi James, I was wondering why the house was so dark."

"Thought I'd surprise you since I have to leave for a while tomorrow."

"Cooper dragging you on another suicide mission?"

"Ellery you know what I do helps pay for our life."

"Yes, I know James. Yet you won't tell me exactly what it is that you do."

"I told you I'm a private security contractor." James spoke quickly.

"James you say that but when you come home it feels like you lose part of yourself on each job."

She had no idea how right she was.

"Ell I'm going to retire soon."

"You say that James, but you know the war is over. You don't owe them anything."

"Can we not do this right now?"

"It's never a good time to talk about it."

Ellery stood up and walked out onto the dock. He followed closely behind. As tears flooded down her face, she felt two hands rest on her shoulders and a kiss against the back of her head.

"Look I'm sorry sweetheart. When I get back after this assignment, I promise I'll tell you anything you want to know."

"Really James?"

"Cross my heart."

They finished their dinner and held each other until the sun came up.

It was time for him to go. Time for him to depart on a journey that would take another piece of his humanity. He had no choice and that is what bothered him most. Making a deal with the devil is never as glamorous as it seems. All those materials and paper currencies would not restore what he had fed to the darkness.

Society was becoming a monster of industrialism and profits. His role was to feed that monster and help it grow bigger until no one could put it down. He took one last look at her while she slept. A tear came to his eye as he painted a mental picture of her in his memory. He kissed her on the head and shut the door. Walking down the stairs he heard a little voice speaking.

"Daddy?" Ellie spoke.

"Daddy will be home in a few days, and we can go pick flowers together" James replied.

The little girl jumped and danced with joy before running to hug her father.

"Okay I love you daddy."

"I love you too princess" he said struggling to fight back the tears. He closed the front door and took the first steps to his demise.

CHAPTER 3-

His phone vibrated as he stepped off the private jet. A message from cooper.

-2314 harrows lane-

Another job. Another check to keep his way of living secure. That is what he had to tell himself to be able to do what he does. It is for the greater good. James had a driver waiting for him outside the gates. A man in all black opened the door for him. As the driver got in, he spoke but James could not hear.

"Come again?" James asked.

"Where to agent Grayson?" The driver spoke again.

"Take me to the harvester."

An hour later James arrived at a building that looked like an underfunded city hall. He walked through the revolving doors and the front desk attendant gave him a key. Making his way towards the elevator he glimpsed outside and saw cooper's motorcycle.

The doors dinged as they opened for him. A group of young men walked out past him. They had such brightness and curiosity in their eyes.

"If they only knew in a year that everything, they once thought about the world was a web of lies" he said aloud.

The elevator doors shut, and he inserted the key into a special slot and turned. The screen showed a giant letter H and proceeded downwards.

"Down into the belly of the beast" He told himself once again.

As the doors opened, he saw what he had become so familiar with over the past years. Computers using algorithms to track down civilians who had been deemed "collectable". Every name and face on those screens had been chosen for a specific reason. To be taken and harvested of the one thing that made them unique. Their soul.

"Mr. Grayson" A man spoke.

The voice came from a man who looked like a shady politician. He sported close cropped hair that was receding and a pair of tortoise shell eyeglasses. The suit he wore had to have cost more than most people's cars. His name was Alfred mason. Director of operations for the United States harvesting network. James hated him with every fiber of his being.

Probably due to his lack of a moral compass. James felt remorse about what he did and empathy for those who he drained. Director mason on the other hand loved every single job. He thought the world was plagued by low value civilians and was okay with any method to rid the world of them. A modern-day Nazi.

He had recently assembled a strike force to eliminate "unsavory" characters that could interfere with all the work and money he had invested in the profession of harvesting. Not that most people knew about it anyways. They had gotten their government contract by saying they would run tests on those already in death beds with the family's consent. There was never any consent. They violated a person's rights and in his tower he sat. Watching through screens as the life drained from the eyes of peasants.

James turned to look at the director and shook his head in disrespect of his superior. The computer was analyzing their next target. Faces appeared and disappeared. Like waves forming and crashing during a coastal storm. Then the screen stopped on a man and a woman. Not very often did the computer choose a couple but once the names were highlighted it was set in stone. James and cooper looked at their next targets.

He looked distraught while cooper came around the corner smiling with sadistic pleasure. It was a family. Just like his. Sorrow filled James's heart. Cooper thought of it as practice for what was to come.

"Let's get going James" said cooper with an over excited tone.

"Yea I'll be right there coop."

James looked one last time at the screen. They were a couple in love just like him and his wife Ellery. The pictures displayed were ones of happiness and togetherness. He was about to rob them of everything they had, but most fucked up of all he was going to steal their chances of spending eternity together.

The house was dark when James and coop arrived. The clouds had sensed this horrific tragedy that was about to take place and brewed a storm of violent rain. Lightning flashes illuminated the dark streets while they lock picked the front door. The duo was dressed in all black stealth suits. Night vision eyewear and a suppressed .45 caliber pistol was their gear for their operations.

Coop got the door open and slowly they slipped into the house. Clearing all the downstairs rooms and finally making their way up the stairs. Back-to-back they walked. Just like they did during their tour of Syria. Death was an old friend to them both. As they made it upstairs, they saw the illuminating light of the master bedroom.

Cooper signaled towards the door and James nodded in recognition of the light. Both inserted tranquilizer rounds into their pistols and got ready to breach the room. James turned the knob and slowly pushed the door. Cooper went in first with astonishing speed. Firing two tranquilizers rounds into the woman before she could even scream. The man grabbed a pistol from the nightstand and got a shot off. Cooper put two rounds into his stomach. Out like a light.

"That was a close one James" Cooper laughed

"James?"

In all the chaos he did not see his partner get hit. James slumped against the door frame. The bullet has missed the body armor and hit James in the neck. He took his vest off so he could breathe. He held the wound with one hand and started walking around to check the vitals of their victims.

"It's just a graze coop. through and through" James reassured him.

Before either of them could bag up the targets a voice came from the hallway behind them.

"Mommy? Daddy?" A soft voice spoke.

A little girl stood looking into the room as her parents laid unconscious. James looked at her and almost cried. She looked just like his little princess Ellie. He had just harvested a family. A family just like his.

"Coops leave the bodies. We are going now" James shouted.

"What the fuck are you talking about James?" Cooper spoke bitterly.

"This went all wrong. She saw us and I have been hit. My blood is all over the place."

"No, I will not ruin my work because of your god damn altar boy heart."

Coop switched magazines to live rounds and cocked his gun. James tried to knock the gun away, but he was too late. Cooper aimed his .45 at the little girl and fired. A flash lit up the room. The bullet flowed ever so gracefully towards its target. Sliding through flesh and bone like a hot knife through butter. A clean shot. A life ending shot. The little girl's body fell lifeless on the floor.

"What the fuck is wrong with you coop? She was a little girl" James shouted.

He slammed Cooper against the wall and pinned him with his arm.

"She was expendable. Nothing gets in the way of my work" Cooper explained.

James swung and busted cooper's nose.

"Fuck you coop. I'm in the way of your work now."

Coop pointed his gun at James. The room was completely still. Lifelong friends turned into mortal enemies.

"Do it coop" James taunted him.

"Don't make me pull this trigger James" Cooper said with eyes watering.

"You killed a little girl you are a fucking monster."

"She was in the way. Plain and simple"

"What happened to you brother?"

"You happened to me you son of a bitch. Rubbing all your happiness in my fucking face all the time"

"I let you in my life. In my family's life"

"Well now it's not your life anymore James."

The room went quiet, and James closed his eyes. He opened them to see three holes in his chest with smoke pouring out. So much pain followed by the bite of bitter cold. Cooper stood over him to finish the job but thought he should let him have an open casket. One last gift to his departing friend. Cooper leaned down and whispered in his ear before bagging up the victims and preceding out of the house.

"I'll take good care of them brother" Cooper stated.

James laid there in a pool of his own blood. Saying the names of his wife and daughter one last time before the last breath left his lungs. Dying slowly all, he could see was the little girl laid next to him with a bloody hole between her eyes. She looked just like his daughter Ellie. To see her dead tore apart his heart. A heart that was already shredded by bullets. Killed by the man he trusted most. His vision started to fade as he let out a dying laugh.

"Everything close and comfortable". He whispered.

James closed his eyes and his life slipped away with one last thing on his mind. Revenge.

CHAPTER 4-

James awoke to a grey sky with swirling black clouds. Sitting up to brush the dirt off himself his fingers grazed over the bullet holes coop had left in him. Anger and overwhelming guilt swept over his bullet ridden heart. His survival instincts kicked in and overcame his need for revenge. He stood up and traveled down the lifeless hill he woke up on.

Noticing all the grass and trees were dead or dying. As he was looking down at his footsteps, he noticed the brass plates. Names and dates yet there was no inscriptions. He was in a graveyard. The panic set in as he realized that he must be in purgatory or even worse, hell. Looking up he noticed a skeletal bird flying except when it opened its beak there was no sound. No life.

What a strange place to end up, but James knew he would never end up in what the Catholics and Christians called 'heaven". Surveying the surroundings of this bleak world he came across a street sign with multiple arrows. The signs letters had been replaced with eyes, but each one with a different color. He followed the most comfortable sign. The one that had his own eye color.

The dead grass started to form into rocks then into a path. The path led down to an old empty city. In an instant his mind processed what it was seeing. This was the city where the harvester was, but it had no life. No people. No cars and no sirens. The concrete beast was no longer breathing. A strange noise broke his train of thought.

The sound of cans clinking together and scraping wheels made its way into view. An old man with a rusty shopping cart crossed in front James coughing and wheezing. He was homeless. Then again as of now James was too.

"Excuse me sir" he said to the old man.

The frail man turned only to reveal a skull and long beard infested with gnats. His mouth opened and past the holes from missing teeth a voice spoke.

"Hey man you got some change?" A shrill old man spoke.

"Sorry man I don't think I do" James said in a confused tone.

"Where are we?"

"All questions have a price my friend, and my price is a coin."

"I'm dead how am I supposed to give you a coin?"

The skeletal man smiled then laughed loudly.

"we all come here with a coin" he chuckled out "check your pocket.

James checked his front pocket, and sure enough there was a coin. He pulled it out to examine it. Finding only an eye on both sides of the coin. James tossed the coin into one of the mans dented tin cans. Only then did he notice the cans all had words on them. He looked closer to see the words written... Faith. Love. Empathy. Hope. Kindness.

James thought for a second on what his question would be. Right as he was about to ask his question the old man started to speak.

"Since you're new to this I'll let you ask two questions. The two questions you are deciding on as we speak." The old skeleton spoke.

"How do you know that I'm deciding between questions?" James asked.

"We all have more than one ultimate question in life do we not?"

The old man started to seem more like an oracle than a street bum. James took a second to decide which question to ask first. Overwhelmed with curiosity he began to speak his first inquiry.

"Why do your cans have those words written on them?" James asked.

"ahh my friend that is a great question, and to answer it the explanation is humanity" The skeleton replied.

"I'm confused" James said dumbfounded by the old man's reply.

"These cans are what the living throw away in exchange for material possessions. What used to be garbage is now important. What was important is now garbage."

So badly he wanted to ask how the fuck he knew his name, but more importantly he needed to know where he was. After all he did wake up in another version of his world where everything was dead. Except an old crazy skeleton who knew more truths than the acid shaman at burning man. What a strange place to end up.

He always imagined he would just wake up after death in a black void with no sound. No light. No warmth. Just the cold to wander in forever. He had no religious affiliation so what was the point of believing in life after death. Life was already just moment after moment of death. If its not yours its someone's else's.

Yet his mind wandered back to the cans and the coin. The same eye on the coin appeared on the street signs. That is when he noticed the the grating on the old mans shopping cart. Along the side was black spray paint dripping down onto the wheels. The black lines forming into an eye. Except this eye was not opened. It was closed.

The old man was not letting onto to his true motives, but this wasn't the time to go making enemies with the only other life or type of life he's seen since he awoke. James took a breathe and started to walk toward the cart.

"I have my question" James said with a stern tone.

"Then ask your question."

James thought one last time on what he was about to ask. He needed to know where he was. How he got here. Where to go. Unfortunately, the only thing he wanted to ask was why the old mans eye was closed. A question that could be useless and then he'd be left to wander this world forever. Always curious and maybe never seeing another person to ask a question to for eternity. He decided with an absolute resolution in his mind.

"Why is your symbol of the eye closed?" James asked.

The old man's skeletal jaw hung open. He used his boney hand to close it back and began to stand straight. James could see clearly how large the man was after he stood straight and shrugged off his cloak. He had to be seven foot tall or taller. Within his rib cage laid a black heart pumping dark fumes into a series of tubes that acted as his circulatory system. There was no way to tell how old this man truly was. Chips in his bone frame suggested he had seen many battles with arrows and blades.

The old skeletal figure looked into James eyes and spoke in a deep voice. Behind the deep voice followed the voices of so many others. Both male and female. Young and old.

"We are those who will not watch as you steal our souls" a little girl's voice spoke.

"We know but do not act until now" said the shrilled sounds of an old man.

"We linger but do not show ourselves" a tortured woman cried out.

The sky grew pitch black. Wind whipped with the stench of death.

"We will no longer sit idle while humanity steals our very life force" The voices all spoke in unison.

James panicked as he realized this might be hell after all. That he was about to be tortured for all the suffering he caused in the name of personal gain. He began to step back and try to run. It proved useless. The fumes from the skeletal colossus had traveled onto the ground and wrapped James legs like dark tentacles. The fumes smelled like violet but carried hints of death and decay. James already dead body went colder than he thought possible. His eyes began to change colors and his brain filled with images of his victims.

The skeletal mass spoke with its choir of tortured voices.

"The souls you take. The lives you rip from this earth will be given back. You will help us James Grayson for you know how to steal life, and now you shall return it" They spoke in unison again.

The last vision James saw was through a strangers eyes. A rooftop. Sirens blaring in the background. The stranger was looking at the sky, but it was not the normal sky. It was a kaleidoscope sky. Then he could feel what the stranger was feeling. A heartbeat. Happiness. It felt like an eternity since he experienced those things.

As the vision was ending the stranger looked at a broken piece of glass. The reflection showed a young man in his early twenties. long hair and shaved sides. Tattoos. Then a name was spoken loudly in both James and the strangers minds.

Iris.

CHAPTER 5-

The spiritual journey he was so wrapped up in came to a screeching halt. Hearing his name being spoken so clearly by an ethereal voice sobered him up immediately. Iris turned to notice the stranger who had given him this life altering substance was gone. Vanished into midair. Only leaving behind confusion and regret in iris's mind.

Hoping he had not just caught some sort of disease or virus by using this strangers needle. Realizing he should look for that omniscient syringe he walked the rooftop still coming down from his trip.

Shuffling around he began to hear more voices in his head, but these were not of his name. The voices were almost like someone's memories playing through headphones in his ears.

The sound of a little girls laughter followed by the words "I love you" in a woman's soft voice. Freaking out iris began to converse with himself. He tends to do that under incredible amounts of stress or confusion.

"Iris its all good man just breathe" he said aloud.

"fucking losing my shit here dude" he remarked back to himself.

Hoping laying down would bring this day to end he began to walk back down the stairwell to his floor. He walked to the door to the apartment only to find he had locked himself out. Luckily, iris had a group of shady friends when he was growing up. He pulled his ID out of his wallet and slid it into the seam of the door. A few swipes up and down.

A couple pushes and pulls of the door. Beautifully it swung open without a dent on his ID card. A smirk crept across his face as he felt dangerous for lock picking the door. Then again that is the least dangerous thing he had done today. Making his way toward the tiny bathroom to check his skin for blood marks he began to hear voices again.

This time there was so many he could barely make out what they were saying. Like a public forum or town hall meeting it was just voices talking over one another without any regard for the other sounds. So close he was to his bathroom yet so far it seemed. Things began to slow down all around him. His ear drums were battered with vibrations.

Losing balance, he made one last ditch effort to get into the bathroom. Running forward he pushed past the door and fell directly onto the cold tile haven he had so direly been seeking. On that frigid linoleum his head laid. Iris stared up at the leak stain ridden ceiling hoping he could see right through it. Back to the kaleidoscope sky. Back to the happiness and warmth he had once felt. Feelings so unfamiliar to him.

"I need to get stoned" Iris said aloud.

Once the sickness from the stem comedown began to dissipate, he was able to regain enough strength to stand. Gaining his bearings, he taught himself how to walk again. A grown infant struggling with his first steps to his parental weed stash. Iris finally got back to normal human like movements. Shuffles advanced into footsteps. Footsteps that led him to the false siding of his kitchen pantry.

Reaching his hand up he pulled a string from a faulty lightbulb switch. A piece of wood proceeded to slide out of place behind the collection of cereal boxes. Iris had a profound love for cereal. Cereal the life source of your average stoner. Like the promised land of milk and honey. Stoners had chips and cereal.

Iris friends were amazed at his stash spots all over his apartment as well as the city. Then again that was how he made a living. Selling the dankest of buds to his friends and anyone that needed. The all-natural medicine that was somehow ranked just as bad as heroin. Iris could go on for hours about the politics behind the war on drugs and marijuana reform. Right now, though he just really needed to get baked. Like real baked.

That kind of high when you can barely keep your eyes open. The type of stoned that when you are in public everyone knows you are baked, and you do not give a single fuck. He needed that level of lifted. So, iris began to collect his specimens out of their glass jar habitats.

Like Charles Darwin discovering new species of animals across the world. Iris traveled far and wide to collect the most pure and exotic strains of bud. Crazy colors and structures followed by even crazier names. Alaskan thunder fuck. Purple Nurple. T.I.T.S(this is the shit). Grand wizard blueberry.

"Who the fuck names these" Iris said aloud while laughing.

Deciding to go to the highest plain of marijuana existence his conscious could achieve he grabbed all the jars he had. Lining them up on the table like revolutionary soldiers getting sent to the slaughter of cannon fire. Next to the jars his collection of glass stood tall. Bongs, bubblers, pipes, steamrollers, vapes. Iris was a true connoisseur and purveyor of the cannabis world.

Searching through his couch he found the remote to his sound system. Buttons covered in sticky weed residue and Cheetoh prints he pressed play. Relaxing alternative music began to play through the apartment. "Just Dumb" by boy and bear. His favorite song of all time.

Something about the notes and lyrics reached deep inside him. Let him feel at peace in his chaotic world for the five minute and thirteen seconds it played. Iris relaxed his shoulders, laid his back, and opened his ears. Letting the tones give him a natural rhythm he interlaced his fingers together and cracked his knuckles. Showtime.

He pulled out the grinder he called "schoolhouse" which was just a regular weed grinder but with a classic pencil sharpener crank on top. To assist with breaking the stick icky of course. He methodically began to open each jar and take a single large bud out of each one. Setting each bud out in front of their corresponding homes. He ground each one up and rolled a joint. Packed a large bong bowl. Loaded the vape. Then it was blast off. Smoke emanated off his living room table like a California wildfire. Clouds rolling off onto the floor. Fog machines at Disney land density in his clouds. Once all was said and done Iris sat there thinking. Flashing back to what he saw when the stem first hit. The rush of colors and sound. The rush of his heart for the first time in recorded history. Not even sex gave him that feeling. The bliss he achieved in that moment was unlike anything he ever thought he would experience. Now it was gone just like the stranger who offered it.

Iris sat there thinking and smoking for hours. Switching artists and albums as he meditated in marijuana for the rest of the evening. High as shit but still could not shake the memory of his voice being said to him like that. Like it had been whispered in his ear. Making the hairs on neck stand up from the closeness.

His phone began its usual vibrating at the same time each night. Time for work. A multitude of inquiries and orders came in. People asking what he had in stock and the accompanied prices. Iris pulled up a floorboard underneath the table to reveal a scale and bags.

The next thirty minutes or so was spent weighing out, labeling, and sealing packages. Iris liked to give everything a personal touch, so he wrote nick names on the packages and put a corresponding mark depending what time of year it was. He put on his sweater and jeans. Slipped into his pumas and threw his laptop bag over his shoulder. He used it as cover when carrying product because it had a false smell proof bottom, he sowed into it. If a cop searched the bag, they'd only find the laptop and charger.

Remembering to grab his key Iris made his way out into the hallway. Locking his door, he waved hello at his elderly neighbor Dorris. She had stage three cancer and no family or money for chemo. Iris gave her free product to help with keeping food down as well as pain management. If he was going to do something illegal, he might as well give back to the world. He was not one to sit and watch someone suffer. After making it down the stairwell to the lobby he reached behind the mailboxes and grabbed his longboard. Not a fan of the regular skateboard because of its inability to go over sidewalk cracks and also his own lack of balance.

He prefers to ride smooth and fast on the pavement. Street surfing and curving around corners at incredible speeds. Hills welcome a sense of fear and the chance to cheat death. Iris wears no helmet for he does not fear death. Only protection he needs against the carnivorous asphalt is his clothes and his slide gloves. Essentially just gloves with hockey puck shaped rubber circles on the palms. They helped with the sharp turns where he had to lean his entire body weight against the curve to be able to make it without eating shit.

Iris pushed his headphones into his ears and the music began to play. This time his start song of choice was "Caring is Creepy" by the shins for its upbeat pace. He looked down and then back up. Pushing off on his left foot and balancing on his right he began to coast. Picking up speeds with consecutive foot pumps and riding gravity down hills he began to blaze throughout the city streets.

Observing humanity at a blur is an interesting take on life. To see it all so fast and try to process it just as quickly. The music in his ears replacing the words of his fellow human beings. All the shouting. The cries and the laughter drowned out by his own selection of tones. Almost like he was watching a slideshow where the projector is flicking through images too fast. Pieces is he all he sees at those speeds.

Fragments of emotions. Wishing he could feel their sorrows and joys for more than the split second he had with stem. This was his was television. Channel surfing through the passerby view of peoples woes.

After an hour or two of destination skating and covert ops weed transactions Iris was finally on his last delivery. It was getting to be the time of night when you do not want to get caught outside holding by the police or even worse. Jack crews. Groups of thieves who take what he and other dealers work hard for. Everyone has their hustle, but some require no respect or value.

Making his way down the hill a screeching noise broke through his headphones. The voices calling his name started again and they were so much louder this time. He took the headphones out to see if he was imagining it, but still the voices sang in his ears. Irritated this happened right before his last stop he pushed onward. Except with every push of his foot the voices grew louder and louder. Then the vibrating began in his ear drums. His balance was gone. Iris lost control of his board and when he finally looked up went headfirst into a tree branch.

Laying on the ground and losing consciousness all he could see as he drifted away was an eye. An eye that burned into his mind like a cattle brand.

CHAPTER 6-

Waking up to a swirling sky for the second time that day James still could not get familiar with his new world. He sat up only to see the colossus was gone. Lingering purple smoke trails and the smell of lavender was all that was left of the skeletal man. Yet one tin can lay on the ground next to James. He picked it up to read the inscription "Family".

He fell to his knees clutching his broken heart while he cried out the name of his wife. The undead guide to this world had left him that tin can remind him what he threw away. His family was all he wanted, but his need to know if the grass was greener on the other side robbed him of them in the end. James began to contemplate just sitting there forever. Letting the centuries roll by as he held that tin can to his chest. Suddenly a voice broke his painful silence.

"Don't cry mister" a little girl spoke empathically.

"who said that?" James asked.

"Me over here sir"

James opened his eyes only to be horrified by what stood in front of him. It was her. The little girl from the house. She stood there dressed in blood-soaked pajamas. Her forehead adorned with a cauterized bullet wound.

"How are you here?" James asked terrified.

"we all come to this place" She answered

"who's we?"

"the ones with no souls"

James let a putrid tear run from his ducts. He wondered how she ended up here when her brain was dead from the shot coop had let off. She should have never made it to the harvester.

The little girl laughed and skipped around the concrete streets. Singing to herself.

"Ring around the rosy. Pocket full of posies. Ashes, ashes. We all fall down."

She turned to James and laughed.

"We all fall down James. We all fall down." She spoke quietly.

Then just like that she fell. Lifeless she lay there just like she was when James saw her in his last moments of life. The cauterized wound on her head began to glow then changed to a scar in the shape of an eye. Losing his fucking mind, he began to run.

In no direction and with no destination he just ran. He realized in death you do not grow tired or feel pain. Simply because you are dead of course. He ran for miles throughout the empty city looking for some sign of life. Hours of searching proved fruitless.

He had made his way all the way to the top of a highway overpass when he saw smoke coming out from under a bridge. Of course, he had to investigate. Even if he found nothing at least the smoke probably came from a flame which might help warm his cold cadaver bones. James made it to his destination only to find an old campfire and tent under the bridge.

He sat down next to the fire only to get the smell of burning lavender. He closed his eyes trying to picture his daughter and wife. Maybe a small memory could stop his suffering inside even if only for a moment. Nothing appeared. Its like the memories were there but the video player in his head would not project them. Opening his eyes, he saw the shopping cart once again, but this time it was down at the bank of a river next to the bridge.

Shuffling around in the grass was the skeletal hobo once again. This time he was cursing obscenities while trying to patch a leaky canoe with glue and newspaper. James found the whole scenario to be quite comedic. The man or monster who let him stay confused and lost was now having his own issues. Thinking maybe now was a good time to get on the hobo's pleasant side James walked up to offer his help.

"Looks like you could use a hand old friend" James shouted.

"I've got two hands but as you can see, they are a bit boney" the skeleton man laughed hysterically at his own pun

James lifted the canoe above his head as the skeleton patched the holes. The "glue" he had used smelled like formaldehyde.

Wanting to ask why he used that James began to answer his own question. What other kind of sticky substance would you find in the land of the dead. Things started to seem less evil and more mysterious in this land of gray. The lavender smell became pleasant to the new resident of this world. A sort of Stockholm syndrome. This place captured him, and he might as well fall for it. It was going to be all he would ever know for eternity.

"Want to go for a ride down stream?" the skeleton asked.

"fuck it why not" James said throwing caution to the dead wind.

They put the canoe in the water, and both got in. The skeleton handed James an oar and they both began to row. The water was calm, and the city looked somewhat peaceful from far away. Drifting and floating around the realm of the dead. A river of death. As that thought crossed his mind, he saw something in the water.

Looking down he could see right under the murky surface. It was a person swimming in the current, but not a regular person. They had no shape to them only the face. The rest was just a floating mass of energy or life. Or lack thereof.

"They're the ones with no destination. The ones you robbed of fate" the skeleton spoke.

James sat and thought about that statement for a long while. If they could not get in heaven or hell, then this must be purgatory. Meaning James had not been judged yet for his sins. Neither good nor bad he was in the grading phase.

He wanted that extra credit to earn his way up. Even if he were not a believer maybe heaven would let him have his memories of his family again. Pieces began to click together in his mind like a puzzle. The old skeleton with the knowledge. The river. The swimming lost souls. He thought a name and, in that name, came clarity.

"Charon" James said to the old man.

The skeleton turned and nodded in agreement. He was the ferryman from the days of old. The time of gods and myth. James was between worlds now. In front of him sat one of the oldest beings of time. The final friend before the journey into agony. He knew it right then. His destination was hell.

Atonement for his sins in the burning fires of despair. Yet he did not feel scared. He deserved it in his own mind. The river he drifted on was the one and only river styx. They made their way down the stream for hours until the dead city disappeared amongst the swirling gray skylines. Floating onward to the gates of hell.

"You're not on your way to eternal hellfire just yet James" Charon spoke aloud.

"Then where am i going?" James asked.

"you've still got time to fix the wrongs you've made. Return the souls you stole".

"How?"

A section of the stream ahead began to split into two paths. One with pillars of fire and one with twisted roots forming into an eye. An overgrown forest cut in half by the water. The path less traveled they took.

"Before you can begin to fix what you have done you must first suffer. Every act of heroism comes with sacrifice James." The skeleton spoke these words.

He spoke the words without optimism. He spoke them with regret and empathy. For what was about to come would deal the final blow to James's already broken heart.

CHAPTER 7-

Iris awoke from his skull crushing wipeout. Ears ringing and a mouthful of blood he slowly started to stand. He was in excruciating pain, but the voices had stopped. What a trade. Concussion and possible irreparable brain damage just to make the voices go away. Just to make them stop shouting his name in his head. Iris dusted off his pants and shirt while looking around.

Scanning the area to see if anyone had seen him wreck shit on his board. It seemed like no one had noticed, and if they had they did not give two fucks. From the outside eye Iris is just like every other skater punk or hipster millennial. To the drug knowledgeable he was just a pot dealer. In his mind he did not know how to describe himself. Every time he looks in the mirror its a different stranger. Like the glass was a window to another dimension of look alike drifters and travelers.

An existential crisis is a real bitch and a half to deal with. An inner war with your own soul or lack thereof. Constantly hating yourself for what you have or have not done up until now, but the only thing you want to do is love who you are. Its not having your cake and eating it too. Its the fucking farthest thing from it. Like having a cake, but right when you want to eat it the thing disappears entirely from your memory and all existence. Then you see that cake all around in everyone else's life but cannot remember why it seems so familiar. Why everyone can have theirs, and yet you can not.

That is an existential crisis. Not knowing why everyone can enjoy their "life". While the concept of it just does not make any fucking sense at all. Iris had told many different shrinks his thoughts on "life". That only got him a list of "specialists", and a trash bag of zombifying pill bottles. Big pharmaceutical doing their part as always.

Iris contemplated suicide a handful of times as a young adult. Then at one point he just thought thats too easy. He needed to stick it to the man. Die fighting the system even if it boiled down to just peddling some grass. Roll the dice.

Zoning back out of his thoughts and zoning in towards reality he noticed his last sack for delivery was missing. He began to search near the base of the tree he ran into. Piles of leaves were being assaulted by garbage swept around with the coming breeze. Finding a plastic bag amongst trash is like finding a needle in a haystack. Iris tried using his sense of smell which he thought was pinpoint accurate. Due to all his years around weed of course. He finally stumbled across his plastic bag laying under a pile of tin cans. In the 21st century it is not often you had come across tin soup cans. Everything was aluminum now anyways.

As he bent over to retrieve his stash, he noticed the cans had words written on them. The words themselves were somewhat profound to be written on such a worthless piece of garbage. Iris had more important things to tend to then be pondering over some cans with words on them. He put the weed in his laptop bag while making sure no one was looking. Last thing he needed right now was to be dealing with some overzealous police officer.

Iris made his way back up to the street to find his board. After a few moments of surveying the area he saw the board in the distance. It had rolled at least a few hundred feet. He made his way too it, and upon arrival checked for any major damage from the impact. The nose was chipped a little, but nothing too serious.

Essentially it is just a piece of wood so no harm no foul. Iris messaged his last client to let them know he was going to be running a tad late. It proved difficult to keep his balance atop his board, so walking was the only option. He figured he could reach the clients home in about fifteen minutes of walking, so he began his short journey. Upon arrival to the two story victorian town home he rang the buzzer at the gate. There was a chime than a voice spoke.

"Dr. Redford residence. State your manner of business." an older gentleman said with a no-nonsense tone.

"Iris for Dr. Redford" Iris stated

"Very good sir please do come in" The butler replied.

The gate opened and Iris made his way up to the front door. He was greeted by the older butler who had a subtle southern accident. As the butler opened the door for Iris, he noticed a collection of strange plants and flowers on the front porch. Walking into the entry he could not help but look up and marvel at the architecture.

He had been here over fifty or sixty times yet the roman pillars and century old crown molding on the ceiling remained elegant. The house had to have cost millions of dollars just in itself not including the real estate location. At the top of the stairs stood Dr. Redford or as Iris called him "Red".

"Whats up homie" Red said with a gangster tone.

Iris laughed at how idiotic it sounded when Red said that. Probably because Dr. Redford or "Red" was a forty-five-year-old balding white man with a gut.

"Whats up brother" Iris replied with an over exaggerated tone.

"Hey, my man don't hate appreciate. One love" Red said sounding confused with his own words.

"Why do you talk like that dude?"

"I don't know Iris I'm trying to relate to my younger patients" He said exhausted.

"Its all good man" Iris reassured him.

Red had been a doctor for twenty-five years. A genius in the medical field and an appreciator of psychological studies as well. He had found marijuana in medical school when the stress became too much for him. Studying the exact medicines, he would be prescribing he knew the side effects would ruin his body.

So, Dr. Redford began to study the whole spectrum of medicine. From eastern remedies to spiritual healing. He traveled abroad to learn how much the body can take and respectively how much it could heal from. The human body was the perfect self-sufficient bio-organic machine on earth. Red wanted to master this machine and help fix those who had defects in their own.

Marijuana had proven to help with so many of his patients symptoms on a broad spectrum that he became one of the father figures of the medicalization movements. Iris had met him through a rally to end marijuana prohibition. They had been buddies ever since. Red was also his best customer since he believed Iris had the best stuff available in the city.

Iris thought he should clear the doctors bill for services rendered by offering a trade of sorts.

"Hey doc you think we could call our bill even and you give me a check up?" Iris asked.

"Sure, what's up man?" The doctor replied.

Iris began to tell Red of the evening before. The stem and the stranger. The voices. The feeling of happiness. He spilled the beans entirely to the doctor while he listened and read through some textbooks. Trying to find explanations on the drug as well as the side effects. They sat there for over an hour exchanging his experiences as well as handing joints back and forth to each other.

"Psychoactive substance. LSD type visualizations. With MDMA type euphoria. Fascinating. Truly fascinating." The doctor spoke.

"Ive never felt anything like it man, and I've been to fucking burning man" Iris said proudly.

The doctor began to dig deeper in the back of a bookshelf uncovering old medical books. He pulled them out and blew the dust off them. Expecting moths to fly out the pages once they were opened. He began to read through texts in other languages. Herbal and spiritual apothecary. Tomes of old wisdom meant to stay in their parts of the world.

"Ahh here's something" The doctor shouted with excitement.

The doctor began to read aloud the text describing a nazi era drug. It was supposed to cure the terrible depression of a SS general's wife. Supposedly some soldiers had found the formula amongst a cave when building a bomb shelter.

The mixture described was said to contain the essence of life itself. The tome began to describe horrifying extraction methods. As well as detailed encounters of people who had taken the medicine not being themselves or claiming to be someone else entirely.

"This is some fucking crazy shit dude" The doctor said laughing.

"That doesn't explain the eye i saw" Iris said angrily.

"You mean like this?"

The doctor held up the tome to show Iris the symbol of an eye on the page. The ink born eye stared at Iris. Burning in his mind from the withered page.

CHAPTER 8-

As they floated down the stream that cut between the wood James felt relief. He did not have to spend eternity getting tortured just yet. Charon began to whistle a song as he rowed with his decaying arms. James wondered if he was such an important figure along the journey of death why he would not have been given something to make him look better. Maybe even a shave would help. Then again, his jaw was all bone. The world around them became less bleak and more mystifying. It seems James was on his own odyssey now. His crucible in the arena of fate.

"I advise you not to look into the water my friend" Charon spoke.

James dismissed his warning thinking he could handle some more floating souls. Except this time when he investigated the water it was crystal clear. He could see past the riverbed. His view kept traveling deeper through the water until he looked upon a graveyard full of people. The sky was blue and had clouds bursting with rain.

People dressed in black gathered at a grave atop a hill. It all looked so familiar. Then he realized it was the graveyard he woke up on when he first arrived here. Except this was it in the realm of the living. His eyes shifted to a woman and her daughter sobbing over the edge of the casket being lowered. It was his wife and his daughter.

James began to scream their names at the top of his lungs. His face turned red from all the yelling. There they were. So close but so fucking far away. What kind of torture was ahead if this was just the beginning of the journey.

As he cried and shouted, he noticed a man walking up to his family. It was coop. He wore a mask of sorrow over his treacherous face. He wept and comforted James's loved ones.

The man who murdered him and a little girl in cold blood was standing over his grave reciting fictitious words of dismay. He chanted the lies like he had rehearsed them a thousand times over. His wife laying her head on his shoulder while James watched from afar and suffered.

All the sudden the entire view of it all was ripped from his eyes. He awoke with Charon pulling his head out of the water. Throwing him back into the canoe the skeleton began to shout.

"I fucking told you man. Don't look in there" Charon shouted.

James began to listen as Charon told how the part of the water, they were traveling on was called the Pools of Reflection. The waters were said to have been bathed in by a blind oracle from the time of creation. A blessing and a curse. Even a small flask could be poured into a chalice to show all sorts of things.

It was the downfall of many empires and greedy rulers. This world contained more than just death. The world of the living had advanced so far out of the age of belief and myth that it all vanished. Locked away here. He was in the fucking twilight zone. James grew tired of these trials. Having no hint to what awaited him at the end.

He began to ask Charon many questions about the world he was in and how it was linked to the one he was from. The conversation ranged from science to religion. Past and future. Living and the dead. It all had the same system.

"So why am i doing this and not just going to hell?" James asked.

"Well i guess you could say you are righting a wrong" Charon replied.

The ancient Charon began to tell James of how there was always a balance between worlds. The omniscient and the cursed could only meddle in the world if they abided by an ancient code. Overtime man became advanced and killed off many of the monsters of the past. Keeping the findings locked away forever. Never to surface to the public eye.

He explained how stealing someones soul and turning it into a substance for profit was breaking the code in every way. He ranted about the nazis and their experiments with gypsy witchcraft. James never knew his line of work had such mystical origins. How he and nazis had something in common made him disgusted. Charon then started to explain a young man.

How this young man was somehow the first one to use this godly substance in over seventy years. This young man was the key to ending it all. With doubt in his mind James thought of how much funding the harvester had. How much power his superior had. They could manufacture this into a drug. Sell it to the masses and ultimately be bigger than the government itself.

"How am i supposed to help? I just retrieved people." James stated.

Charon answered with a long series of one worded answers and riddles. Then he snapped out of his jester attitude and back into his self. He began to tell James how he was to play a large role in a series of events. How he was going to return to the world of the living. His body was buried. He could never go back as himself. He would never be who he was. Not as a whole anyway.

He thought how any of this could make sense. He thought back to his brief studies on religion. The only explanation he could think of was some sort of possession. The idea of it was twisted. Only demons and tortured spirits were supposed to possess people. Then again everything he thought about the after life was not at all as humanity had guessed it.

"So am i to possess someone?" James asked.

Charon laughed loudly and shook his head. He began to tell James that his essence would be transferred into a vessel. That vessel being a human yes, but not in a sense of possession. The person he transferred to would still be themselves, but James was to be a guide of sorts. Lending his knowledge and sometimes expertise in the form of motor functions to his vessel.

The whole process made no fucking sense at all. Then again nothing did anymore. James sat and listened to his newfound sensei. Walking him through the history of spirit transfer. How to explain it to he vessel once they realized someone else was in their mind. His mission. His targets. The end goal. It was like he was going on an assignment all over again.

Charon spoke names that James had heard in passing conversation at the harvester. Locations that were supposed to remain secret to all but a select few. Charon knew more of James career than he knew himself. He began to realize what he had been doing was upsetting the balance of things. Forces bigger than the human spectrum were being angered. This was a way to try and restore order.

James thought to himself of how he could redeem himself for his past through this new task. Like a disgraced knight trying to win back his honor. His thoughts were interrupted when Charon spoke a name that shook James to his core. Rattling the ice in his dead insides. It was Cooper. It seems the universe wanted to balance things out. So did James.

He was being given a chance to kill the traitor he once called a brother. James would do it slowly. He wanted to watch the life leave his eyes. Either by his hands around his throat or a blade through his heart. James wanted to see the whites as cooper's vision rolled over welcoming death. He trusted him and let him in. Only to be repaid by having everything he loved stolen from him.

James told Charon that he would carry out this task without question or doubt. That he would kill everyone on his list. Destroy every harvester. Bring the whole fucking thing down to ashes and cinders. He had been betrayed by the ones he trusted. This was his retribution.

His catharsis used to be building. Now it was to be dismantling. From the bottom up. He vowed to charon he would use this chance to return things to how they used to be. Restore the natural order of things. Even if James had to go to hell, he could kill Cooper. Keeping his family safe. To hunt down and kill the wolf. The wolf in sheep's clothing.

The canoe drifted for what seemed like hours. Though the concept of time is not really important once you are already dead. Charon and James talked of their pasts. Achievements and misdeeds. It seemed Charon was once a human just like James was. Thousands of years before he had been killed in battle and woke upon the river Styx. There a being waited to take him to hell. Charon did not want to go so he fought back. Somehow conquering it he had to take his place. He said it was a curse worse than hell itself. It was a disease to him. Having to take people to their eternal destination of suffering. Lying to them telling them its not as bad as the church makes it sound. He had been stuck on the river century after century. Instead of his personal suffering he had to endure everyone else's.

The conversation was interrupted by the canoe running aground. They stepped onto a beach of red clay and sand. With each footstep it became harder to walk. The clay was just building up on the bottom of their feet. James started to notice some of his footsteps would turn the beach darker and darker red. Thats when it clicked.

The red was not from the natural color of they clay. It was blood. His footsteps were going deeper each time. Blood pulsing up from beneath the earth. He began to run toward a grassy knoll ahead. When he arrived, he took off his shirt and cleaned the blood off his feet. This place was testing his mind. He died in a pool of blood. Now he was to walk through it.

"Everything close and comfortable" James said to himself.

Charon looked at him. He began to tell James that everything he was experiencing was due to his own life and sins. The world around him was finding his biggest fears and regrets. Manifesting them into his environment. Trying to break him down more and more with every second he stayed. They finally made it to their destination.

On a hill ahead sat a renaissance era hospital. At the door was a dark figure. As they got closer James could finally see the stranger clearly. It was a tall man dressed in black robes. Bandages just as black wrapped around all his skin. His face was covered by a white mask with a giant beak of sorts. He had seen the mask before. It was a plague mask from the days of the bubonic plague.

"Ahh so this is to be our savior" The plague doctor said while coughing painfully.

"Yes, he's our last hope now" Charon replied.

James walked into the doors of the collapsing hospital. He took a seat in an old waiting room while Charon and the doctor conversed. Occasionally they would look back at James and shake their heads in disagreement.

Tired of being judged James stood up and walked around. Exploring the parts of the building that seemed safe to travel through. He came upon a room with a bed made clean. No dust or debris. Like time and life stood still in it. He entered the room only to discover some sort of electric chair device in the corner. Instead of wires it had tubing that all ended at singular vial. Some sort of extraction chair. He heard the plague doctors coughing behind him.

"That chair has been waiting for someone like you to sit in it for a very long time" The doctor spoke.

The doctor explained the purpose of the chair. The reason for the tubes and the vial. If James was hearing him correctly then this chair was an archaic way of extracting souls. Prototype one of the machines used at the harvester. He had never seen them operate. That was not his job to do. He just delivered the lambs to the slaughter.

Karma is a real bitch. James now must go through the very pain he had subjected his victims to. Then he began to smile. He is dead. He thought there is no way it could hurt him now. He sat in the chair and the doctor began to unravel the tubing. Wrapping it around certain parts of the chair more than others. Using gravity to pull and push. Old school medicine ladies and gentlemen.

The doctor wheezing through his mask took an old needle out of his robe. Except this needle was about the length of the dagger. It had to have been made of brass. It had small Latin engravings all over it.

The doctor began to chant something inaudible. He raised his arm and with a quick motion stabbed James in the chest. The needle went through his bones without chipping or breaking them. It drove deep past his lungs. His heart. Deeper than the heart. James finally realized what was going on. They were drawing out his soul. He felt the cold from his body leave. Then he felt a feeling less than nothing. Somehow being emptier than empty. His thoughts floated as his dead body slumped into the chair further.

"Is it ready to be delivered to the vessel?" Charon asked.

"Yes, the time has come." The doctor replied.

Charon put the vial into his jacket pocket. The doctor handed him an old jar which contained some sort of cream. Charon went on a long journey back to the dead city he had first encountered James at. Digging around his shopping cart full of tin cans he found a piece of paper with an address on it. Cross referencing the address with the street signs he finally made it to his destination. It was an apartment building downtown.

Charon opened the doors and walked past the mailboxes towards the stairs. He made his way up a few floors to a doorway. The door was burned off and the empty apartment had piles of ashes everywhere. Charon sat on the floor and began to open the cream. He rubbed it all over himself.

With each section of body, he lathered his skin was returned to its living state. He looked human once again. Putting the vial with James soul in one hand and his coin in the other Charon began to mutter some Latin to himself. The coin glowed and he was gone.

A few moments later Charon appeared in the same apartment. Except this time, it was furnished. No ashes or burns. He was in the land of the living. Knowing the cream's effects would only last so long he looked for pen and parchment to write a message for someone. He tripped over a pile of clothes and fell to the ground.

That was the first time he had felt pain in a long time. It was nice. He felt alive again for a moment. Charon saw what looked like a writing utensil and paper. He wrote a note for someone.

-Another taste of happiness-

Charon signed the note "your friend from the rooftop". Drew an eye at the top of the paper. Set the vial next to the message. The cream was starting to wear off and Charon began to degrade. His skin was falling off. Once it touched the ground it withered into dust. The coin began to glow again, and he started to drift back to the world of the dead.

"Good luck James" Charon whispered.

Just like that he was gone. James was back in his world again. Only he was just liquid. A substance of his soul.

CHAPTER 9-

He stood there frozen in the room. The eye on the old page held up by Red. Staring at Iris. The symbol resonating deep within himself. In a trance he stood. Having a staring contest with a page of ink. Red pulled his hand down, and just like that Iris was back to reality. He felt a ringing in his ears like an I.E.D. had just gone off next to him. He could see the movement of the doctors mouth, but the words were empty. No syllables or sounds came out. The ringing started to disappear while he slowly began to process the words he was hearing.

"You alright man?" The doctor asked.

"Yea I'm just confused by that fucking eye" Iris replied.

Doctor Red offered Iris a ride home. He was in no condition to skate back to his apartment downtown in the middle of the night. He could suffer another episode or get robbed for skating too close to a street gangs turf. They made their way into the doctors's garage. Clicking the unlock button on his keypad the black Italian sports car blinked its lights. The doors opened upward. Iris always thought it was a bit ostentatious, but the doctor worked hard so he deserved it.

The garage door opened while the car's engine roared. The sound of the acceleration just coming out of the gate made Iris suspect they were about to go extremely fast. Indeed, they went fast. The doctor flew past cars on the road. Occasionally crossing into oncoming traffic to go around people going too slow.

Running pretty much every fucking stop sign and red light. The lights blurred. That is the one thing Iris enjoyed about top speeds in a fast car. The streetlights became like candles. Flickering and bending. They finally arrived back his apartment complex. Red parked in a handicap parking spot, and then proceeded to pull out one of his patients parking passes. Iris glared at him. The doctor replied with just a grin.

Iris stashed his board behind the mailboxes on the first floor. They made their way upstairs to his apartment. While unlocking his door the doctor stood behind him conversing with the elderly neighbor. Making sure the loving old lady was taking care of herself.

The tumbler turned and Iris pushed open the door. They walked into Iris's apartment. The doctor dashed towards the living room couch after seeing the preloaded bong. Red began to rip the bong. Blowing clouds of smoke out and coughing relentlessly.

"Fucking lightweight" Iris said caustically.

"Fuck you man I'm old" The doctor replied while laughing.

Iris sat down with Red and enjoyed a few bowls in his bong. Playing music to drown out his memories of the past twenty-four hours. Everything seemed to have been okay for now. The doctor stood up to retrieve a beer from the fridge when he stumbled across something.

"Hey Iris, you might want to see this" The doctor said.

Iris walked over to the kitchen to find the doctor holding a note. Next to where he had found the note was a vial. Iris snatched the note up and read it. Confused on how the man from the roof knew which apartment he lived in. Even more confused to how the man knew about the eye.

The doctor being a man of science and mystery was interested in the vial. He told Iris he should let him take it home. Test the chemical components. See what they were really messing with. Iris declined. He was already on edge about doing it.

"You know I could technically make this into liquid drop form" Red said proudly.

"So, no more needle?" Iris asked intrigued by the doctors statement.

"Yea you'd just drop it in your eye" He replied laughing.

Iris thought if he should do it again. The come down was fucking harsh last time. Then again, he did feel things so foreign to him it was hard to pass it up. Iris told the doctor to do it. Red made his way to the bathroom. Grabbed some rubbing alcohol and Epsom salt to break substance down.

After tinkering in the kitchen for half an hour or so it was done. The doctor presented Iris with the same vial but with a dropper attached at the top. He told Iris to try it so he could study his state while he was under its effects. Iris agreed. They both sat in the living room. Iris proceeded to lean back. Dropping a dose in each eye. Then just like that he was gone.

The ceiling opened revealing the sky. Constellations he had never seen before formed together and danced in space. He could hear all the sounds of the city, but now instead of ugly tones they were symphonic. Car horns and train sounds played on key beautifully together.

The world had become a sort of heaven. The wind drafts were colorful. Every breeze was multicolored ribbons swimming in the sky. He felt like Hunter S. Thompson. On a hallucinogenic spiritual journey. Everything was as it should be. This was nirvana. This was paradise.

Then just as quickly it became inferno.

All the beautiful sights and sounds were ripped from his view. The chair he was in was being thrown through space and time.

Lights traveled around him until he sat in darkness. He could not move. All there was just his chair. Sitting there.

A gift to whatever shade of death awaited him in this void of nothingness. Then he saw her. A little girl was running around the woods with a man chasing her playfully. She was not scared, and he was not angry. It had to have been her father. The man finally caught up to her and picked her up in the air. The girl laughed and screamed. Enjoying every moment of it.

"I love you daddy" the girl spoke.

Then just like that it was all black again. Except there was a table set up in the woods with candlelight. A woman and the same man sat there. Drinking wine and kissing each other. Iris was losing his shit. Having no idea what he was seeing or who he was seeing.

The last trip was not like this. It was just distortions. These were manifestations. Full auditory and visual hallucinations. He shouted but nothing came out. He was glued to the chair. Having to watch and try to figure out what he was seeing. The scenarios being displayed to him started to speed up and switch out often.

He saw visions of the man in war. His platoon all dead around him and he was the lone survivor bathed in blood. The next vision was that of a dog. Then another of a child being born. A house being built by the man over the years. Then he saw a building. He had seen the building before while he was skating deliveries. It had this ominous creepy vibe to it.

The last vision Iris saw was of the man bleeding out slumped against a door. Another figure stood above him and flashes came from his hand. With the three flashes Iris fell out the chair screaming in agony. Clutching his chest like he had just been shot. He could not breathe. When the pain started to subside, he opened his eyes to see it was all black again except for the man standing above him.

"Hello Iris" The man spoke to him.

Iris stood up and ran into the darkness. The voice repeated itself over and over in his ears. Like it was over his shoulder every time, but there was no sight of this mysterious stranger. Iris finally stopped running to look around. He had lost his chair. Stuck in a void. Like a black hole of sorts. No light yet he could see. Iris heard an exhale behind him.

"Stop running its pointless" The man said sounding annoyed.

Iris stood there staring at this man. He had a military look to him. Close cut hair. Straight posture. Mostly muscle. His eyes carried sadness and anger. His chest had bloody bullet holes in it.

"Who are you?" Iris asked.

James began to explain to him who he once was. Who he is now.

"So, you know the stranger from the roof?" Iris asked.

"Ahh yes that'd be Charon" James replied

Iris looked confused so James began to explain to him everything just the way Charon told him to. He told him of the substance and its origins. How James had been approached by the harvester elite after his service. The people he took. The bigger picture behind what Iris only thought was another street drug. James continued his rant. Trying to get his point across to the young burn out. Iris asked him who the girl and the woman were. James told him of his family and the betrayal.

Told him what would keep happening to innocent people if they did not stop it. Iris was interested in the part about the afterlife interfering with the world of the living. Since he was always curious about death, he was happy to hear there was something on the other side. Iris had never felt a purpose in his life, and just like that he became a pivotal role in the survival of the current world.

James continued to tell him of how he could stay in the back of Iris's mind. Like a voice in his ear to feed him information on their current task. He also mentioned he could take over Iris's body if he allowed it. Allowing him to channel his deadly training into Iris's less than ordinary skill set.

"So, is this permanent?" Iris spoke.

"I'm not sure honestly, this is my first go at this as well kid" James replied.

Iris told James he was ready to do whatever this was. James said okay and reached into his pocket. A coin with an eye was revealed after he opened his hand. He tossed it to Iris. Catching it he could feel the coin tingle his fingers. Warm and cold at the same time. It began to glow. The world around him faded. Iris awoke in his living room to Red staring at him while he wrote on a note pad. He was back in his world. No side effects or voices this time. Maybe it was all just a hallucination after all. The man. The visions. All just a figment of his imagination. It was so vivid though. He could not shake this lingering feeling.

"You alright man?" Red asked in doctor mode.

"Yea I think I'm alright, how long was I out?" Iris asked.

Red explained he was only in a different state for maybe five minutes. He said Iris did not move or stop breathing. He just stared at the ceiling, and occasionally, he would utter an inaudible word. Iris was blown away by what he was hearing.

It literally had felt like he went into the universe. Past the constellations to where it was all black. The void where he met the cosmic stranger who told him of this evil consuming the innocent. It all began to sound farfetched as he recited it back to himself.

"Hey kid don't forget why we're here now" James spoke.

Iris stood up fast and fell backwards toward the wall. Knocking over a bong and breaking it on the ground.

"Hey man not cool" The doctor said seeming upset.

Iris looked around for the source of the voice he heard. It was not Reds. It was the man from his trip. The cosmic stranger from the black hole of memories.

"You weren't hallucinating Iris, I'm right here in your head" James reassured him.

James told him that the vial contained his soul. His very essence. Having ingested him now Iris had become a vessel of sorts. James was a spiritual passenger. The devil and the angel on his shoulders. He could give him his thoughts. His movements. Even his feelings.

That one struck something with Iris. He would be able to feel. Maybe not his own feelings but another persons. A strangers feelings. Then again, his own feelings were a strangers as well. Iris and James had a conversation in his head for a minute while Red just sat there staring at Iris. He was confused at the very least.

"Your friend seems a bit bothered" James laughed aloud in Iris's head.

Iris sat back down. Reassuring Red he was just a having a quick relapse back into the trip. James had told him that he could not tell anyone of what they are doing. If he were to mention James's name and the wrong ears heard it then Iris would become a target.

This had to be covert. Guerrilla tactics. James was about to turn Iris into what some would call a domestic terrorist. If they only knew he had taken on this task to help humanity more than he ever could have before. While also giving the biggest fuck you to the man possible. The step above the government was the shadow government.

The handful that run the world like puppeteers. Pulling the strings of life and death. Creating diseases and drug outbreaks to control the population. He was going to hit their wallet. The harvester had potential to become a multibillion-dollar industry. At that level they could become their own ruling power. Their own religion. Their own god. Now they would become their own downfall. James fueled by revenge and retribution. Iris driven by the greater good.

CHAPTER 10-

Iris sat in his living room staring at the wall. He was no longer who he used to be. Now he was half of a being. A strangers soul occupying his body. A tenant paying a different kind of rent. His currency was emotion. He could feel James in his mind. Not like a physical force. More of the vibe you have when something is watching you.

Through his eyes the stranger watched. An oculus for the dead. They say the eyes are the windows to the soul. In this case they were the windows to two. Iris needed some time alone to process everything so he suggested Red go home so he could get some sleep.

Red obliged and said goodbye. Once the door closed Iris grabbed a mirror and set it in front of him. He sat staring at the mirror seeing if any part of him was different. That is when he noticed it. One of his eyes changed colors. His whole life he had blue eyes. Now one was green.

"That's crazy man you have one of my eyes" James said amused by the discovery.

"I look like a freak" Iris replied.

"No offense kid but the hair and clothes do that on their own."

"Fuck off man."

James began to tell Iris how he would need to change everything about his appearance. His hair would need to be short so he could blend in. Also, so it could not be used against him in a fight. Which James assured him there would be many ahead. He went on how Iris would have to train his body and mind.

James can only give him his moves. His force would not come with it. His muscles were gone, and Iris's little frame could not do much. Over the coming months as they gathered intel on their targets, he would have to become a warrior. A fighter with a purpose bigger than them both.

Maybe even a martyr if the moment calls for it. Dying for a selfless cause was admirable at the very least. His past was to remain his past. He was no longer a pot dealer. No longer a sad sack of self pity. He was reborn. His journey started here. The first step is the hardest, but also the most crucial. Iris walked into his closet sized bathroom. Turned on the flickering light. Opened the drawer by his sink and pulled out some clippers. He looked at the mirror and then proceeded to cut most of his hair off.

He walked out of the bathroom awhile later rubbing his new short hair. The shortened hairs prickled his hands. Yet it was smooth at the same time. He had grown his hair for over two years. All that time spent was just laying on the bathroom floor now. He walked back to the mirror. Removing his shirt, he began to make a mental note of his boney frame. His rib cage was visible.

"God damn get this kid some milk" James shouted out in the corridors of his mind.

Iris chose to ignore the comment. Better not feed the fire he thought. James was kind of a prick. Iris probably would be too if he had lost his family and was murdered by his friend. James began to tell Iris how they would begin his training. It was to be vigorous. Grueling at times. He promised in the end he would feel better than he ever had before physically. He would be strong. He would be fast. He would be deadly.

That is what they needed to face their new foe. A sharp mind and an even sharper dagger. James told Iris to get some rest. For when he woke up, he'd begin his new warrior routine. Iris went to sleep dreaming of memories that were not his. Learning more about James with every vision. Feeling in sync with his new mentor. His ally.

He awoke to a voice shouting in his head. It was James telling him time to get ready. It was not even light out yet. Iris looked at the clock. It read five a.m. and he was not a fan of that time. He slid out of bed to the fridge and grabbed a soda.

Right when he was about to drink it James told him do not even think about it. He explained Iris had to fuel his body like a machine. Clean foods. It would speed up his rate of becoming a weapon. James told him to get out the orange juice and some eggs. He did as he was told. Pouring the juice and eggs into a blender. After that he gulped the chunky mixture down. Trying not to puke from the taste and texture. James explained to him it was good protein source and the acid from the juice kills the raw egg bacteria. Now the training would begin.

Iris dressed up in some loose clothing and began his first of many runs. James said he needed to be able to at least run half a mile without slowing down. That would prove sufficient stamina for the first stage of attack. Iris made it about eighty-five yards before stopping to puke. A shooting pain in his side.

"First time doing this youngster?" James asked.

"Been awhile" Iris replied.

He took a deep breathe and started again. This time he controlled his breathing like James had told him. It became easier. He made it to a plaza filled with metal poles and bars arranged into forms of art. James told him to use them as a workout.

So, Iris looking like a fool began to climb on the art. Doing half ass pull-ups before falling on his face. A security guard was shouting and running at Iris. He was too tired to care. The security guard picked Iris off the ground and started shouting in his face. Something about trespassing and getting arrested. Those words James did not like. Having Iris attract any attention to himself would not be good for their mission.

"Let me handle this" James spoke.

Iris closed his eyes. When they opened again James was in control. He used his feet to propel off the guard's chest. Sending the rent-a-cop into the ground. Iris flipped gracefully back onto his feet. Under control of James, he was a fucking ninja. The guard rushed at Iris again.

This time he swung at his face. James used Iris's arms to block all the attacks. In a fluid movement he brought an elbow to the guards chin. Rippling a shockwave to his brain. The guard stood stunned by the blow. Iris could see his right leg being dragged behind himself. Then it came off the ground with a ferocious speed. The blade of his foot connecting with the side of the guards jaw. Blood and teeth spewed out from his mouth. The man fell to the ground unconscious.

Iris closed his eyes and reopened them. He looked around to see people holding their phones up to record the fight. A police siren could be heard approaching the scene.

"Run kid" James shouted.

Iris took off. Running through the ally behind the plaza. Two officers had made their way on foot behind him. He took a wrong turn and was at a dead end. The officers were yelling with guns pointed telling him to cooperate. Iris closed his eyes. Before they could even open all the way he was jumping onto a ledge above him.

Using one foot he pushed off and jumped to the rooftop parallel of the ledge. He had just scaled a wall in seconds. He was running and jumping over rooftops. The cops running below and using their radios to try to get back up units. After a few minutes he lost them. He stood high on a building. Looking at the city in a newfound way.

One eye green. One blue. Two men with one purpose. He made his way back home using only rooftops. Even if James were in control his body would benefit from the exercise.

He arrived home to see a blur of himself on the news. They called him the plaza ninja. He moved so fast. With such precision. James must have been a terrifying force to fight. He thought how bad the people fucked up to cross him. Iris knew James would not let anything or anyone get in his way.

Not even Iris himself. That is what scared him the most about his new destiny.

CHAPTER 11-

The next two months were filled with routines and schedules that Iris was not used to. His body ached and failed him constantly. James did not exaggerate when he said it would be grueling at times. It fucking sucked.

As each day went on, he could feel himself getting stronger. Getting faster. More agile. He was becoming the weapon James needed him to be. Soon enough the body would be suitable for James to do his work again. Iris began to get looks from girls he would have never gotten before. Could have been the gradual increase in muscle mass. Or maybe the air of danger that Iris now had around him.

Whatever it was he was enjoying it thoroughly. The world around him became his playground. James taught him hand to hand combat in the mirror. Shadow boxing. Iris learned of guns and knives in a very personal manner. They spent almost two hours a day at a shooting range in the country. There Iris practiced until he could master his shot.

All manner of guns were used too. From the small and silent to the big and loud. He was becoming an assassin day by day. Every training regiment made him feel less like a victim. Tired of being weak and ordinary. Now he was unique.

On a particular day running through the city, he stopped waiting at a cross walk. Jogging in place and jamming to the music in his headphones he saw her. The most beautiful creature he had ever seen. She looked graceful in every action she made. Iris could not help but stare. She noticed, but instead of looking away she smiled at him.

"Go get her champ" James spoke quickly.

Iris mustered up the courage to go and talk to the goddess of the crosswalk. As he started to walk towards her a car came flying down the road right at him. Iris could handle this on his own. He pushed the lady next to him out of the way of the car. She screamed for child in the stroller right in the cars path. Iris sprinted towards the stroller and ripped the baby out of the harness. He jumped at the last second before the stroller was crushed by the vehicle. The car then crashed into a street sign. As Iris gave the woman her child before he saw the driver trying to leave the scene. He was stumbling everywhere definitely drunk. Iris ran to him and threw him against his car.

The man shouted drunken curse words into his face. It did not phase Iris. Only made him madder. He began to shout at the driver for almost killing everyone. The driver did not give a fuck at all. Iris raised his fist to strike the drunken fool, but just as he was about to let loose a hand touched his arm softly.

His anger faded and he was himself again. It was the girl from the crosswalk.

"I think you are hero already" She said with a soft Russian accent.

Iris let his arm down and smiled. Dropping the drunk driver to the ground. The girl asked if he would like to go get a cup of coffee. Since he was a hero and all. Iris accepted the invitation and they walked down the street. They walked with their arms intertwined. Iris could smell hints of amber and toasted sugar on her skin.

Whether it was perfume, or her natural scent Iris was intoxicated by it. He could not help but turn his head and stare. She would catch him looking then he would proceed to look away quickly. She thought it was cute he was embarrassed. He had a sense of innocence to him, but at the same time a cape of danger draped over him. She liked it.

"I never got your name" Iris commented.

"Natasha" she replied.

Iris remembered that Natasha stood for Christmas in old Slavic. It was spot on. She gave him that feeling of happiness you would only feel as a child on Christmas morning. A sense of wonder. This peaceful place of solitude could be found in her eyes. They laughed and conversed all the way to the coffee house. As they approached the entrance Iris forgot to hold open the door for her. She did not mind and opened it herself.

"You're why they say chivalry is dead" James spoke in the back of Iris's mind.

"Fuck off grandpa" Iris replied.

An old man turned at him and gave him the middle finger. Iris accidentally spoke aloud instead of in his mind. He had trouble with that lately. Natasha noticing the incident from afar began to walk up.

"What was that about?" She asked.

"Misunderstanding and dementia" Iris said.

They ordered their coffees and sat down. The Russian beauty asked him a multitude of questions ranging from childhood to his future. She was still working on her English, but he thought it was cute. Iris spewed a load of bullshit to her because he obviously could not tell her he was an assassin in training. Let alone like she would believe his story of the soul passenger he had picked up in the backroads of his mind.

Iris changed the subject and began to ask her questions as well. They learned a lot about each other. Well, she learned what he wanted her to know anyway. His life was as secretive as it could get. If the information James spoke was true, then Iris knew more than the government. Possibly most of the world. He was no stranger to conspiracy theories, but this fucking went above and beyond. This was harvesting the essence of life. A soul.

A thing that most people did not even think existed. Now it was this physical substance. You could hold it in your hands. Someones entire life in a little vial meant for LSD. After some time had passed Iris knew he had somewhere to be, so he said his goodbyes. They exchanged numbers and went their separate ways.

Iris arrived at an address that James had written down for him the last time he had taken control. It was by the harbor. Smelled of fish and smoke. Iris never came to the harbor anymore. It was Dragon territory. The Gold dragon clan was the Chinese mafia in his city. They were very low-key but feared publicly.

They had taken control of the harbor by cutting the heads off the Columbian gangsters that used to control it. When the other Columbians went to the dragons den for revenge, they were met with a bullet ridden end. The bodies were dumped at the front of the police station. Just to make a point. Now Iris stood in their domain.

The belly of the beast. He started to attract a lot of angry looks from the workers. They knew he was out of his element. Like a sheep lining up for slaughter. One man saw Iris and began to make a phone call.

"Well kid i hope you speak mandarin or Chinese" James spoke

As Iris tried to turn by a building, he was met with a crew of five men. All of them adorned in dragon tattoos. They wore all black and each had a gun in their hand. One man in all white was behind them. Walking with a cane. As he approached Iris began to see his cane was a katana in its sheath. He had to be the Dragon Head. A rank meant for the most dedicated and elite of members. He approached and said something inaudible in Chinese.

"Hey kid reach in your front pocket and pull out the paper" James explained quickly.

Iris did what he was told. The piece of paper was taken from him by one of the foot soldiers. He proceeded to give it to the man in white. The man studied it for a moment before letting out a long laugh. He then began to speak in english.

"So, you're the one looking for the hardware" The man spoke unsure of who he was looking at.

"Yes sir" Iris replied.

The man was charmed to be called sir.

"most of you people have no respect, but you are different. i like you." the man in white spoke

He gestured for Iris to follow him. They walked into a warehouse full of fish and other sea dwelling creatures. Walking past the assembly line used to gut fish the man opened a hidden door. They proceeded back into a dark hallway with a flickering light.

At the end of the hallway, they came upon a room full of guns. More guns than Iris had ever seen. RPG's, AK47's, C4, Molotov cocktails. These guys had it all. There had to be enough munitions in here to start a small-scale war. A war that the dragons might win. Iris picked up a G28 sniper rifle with a high-powered infrared scope. Next, he found an assortment of kevlar vests and CQC weapons.

"Got a test range?" Iris asked.

"Indeed, we do" the man in white replied.

Iris closes his eyes. James spent the next hour hitting bullseyes with every class of weapon they had to offer. The dragons were overly impressed.

Some of them even asked for tips. Iris was already a hit with the criminal underworld. Here he was kicking it with killers and kidnappers. He was just like them. A resident in the world of shadows.

CHAPTER 12-

Iris stuffed a duffle bag full of explosives, ammunition, and guns. Grabbed a kevlar vest on his way out and threw it over his shoulder. His new dragon friends helped him load the supplies into the SUV he had recently purchased. That was suggested by James. Iris could not wage a war on top of his longboard.

They were getting closer and closer to the first target on their list. His training was about to be use fully for the first time. All Iris knew was that he had to drive a few hours out of town to a remote cabin. James had told him the man on the list had been running from the harvester for years. He was the only man to ever escape it. Due to a doctor not strapping him in well enough and the elevator not being locked down.

The doctor and maintenance man who were careless were never heard from again. Even their families disappeared. Thats the thing about crossing a shadow organization. Something that never existed cannot be blamed for your disappearance.

He thought about maybe going to see his family before this mission. If there was a chance, he was going to die he wanted to get his apologies out first. Give one last goodbye to his parents. Then he remembered the note they ended on the last time they spoke. He changed his mind. They were better off without him. He could never live up to their standards anymore. He was too far gone.

The thing about living in the darkness is after awhile you start to fucking hate the light. Your eyes have adjusted to the void. Monsters play in the dark. The innocent live in the light. He did not know where he fit in anymore. He had not killed anyone, but James had. They were one person now. So did his sins automatically subject Iris to an eternal judgment or was he okay.

They say the soul is judged and not the vessel. Yet without the soul the vessel is just a hollow shell. Without the vessel the soul contains no capacity for action. So, the body must be judged too. Iris could not help but wonder all these things since he accepted James into his subconscious.

The following morning was not the usual regiment of strength and cardio training. It was spent studying maps. Piles of aerial photographs of the cabin laid on the kitchen table. Then Iris noticed the guns from the SUV had been disassembled onto the counter. He had no memory of doing that.

"I should probably tell you i can take control in your sleep" James spoke.

"How long has this been going on?" Iris replied.

James began to tell him of the full extent of the soul transfer effects. That he could only take control when Iris allowed it or when he was dreaming. At that time his subconscious is busy, and James has a window.

"What if i woke up while you were in control?" Iris asked.

"You'd be in my usual position" he explained.

Iris went on to ask what all James had done while he was asleep. Also, how many times he had done this. James reassured him last night was the very first time. Iris seemed unsure about his other half's answer, but it was not time to start losing trust in him now. He began to assemble the guns back together within in record time.

His muscle memory was starting to adapt to the actions James had done. He was relieved to see that he was starting to become useful and did not have to just be a sidekick during the dangerous stuff. To test out his theory he grabbed a knife and threw it a poster on the wall. The blade sliced through the air and landed edge first into the center of the picture. Walking over to pull the knife out he saw he had hit his target.

Between the blade and the poster was a spider. His eyes had seen it and targeted it all the way from the kitchen. It was really happening. He was becoming a bad ass. He thought of all the guys he should have beat up in high school if he would have had these abilities back then.

"enough reminiscing kid" James interrupted.

Iris snapped back to reality and began to study the photographs while assembling his tools. He made himself some food to fuel up. He needed all the energy he could get. As he read the maps, he began to sharpen the blades on the table. Using a tactical knife to slice his eggs and ham. The smell of gun powder and coffee. It was pleasant. It was manly.

He thought of Natasha and how she had stopped him from beating the shit out of the drunk driver. What would she think if she knew he was about to go kill someone. If she had saw all this in his apartment, she would probably call homeland security.

He pushed the thoughts out of his head. Living a double life is hard enough before adding love and lust into the mix. He craved for that attention, but who would be his love and who would be his mistress. Danger or the girl. He was addicted to both.

A few minutes later he was walking downstairs with the duffle slung over his shoulder. The tenants in the complex were all stunned by Iris's transformation. The muscle. The danger in his eyes. They all thought he was just a kind hippie pot dealer. Now they were looking at an operator.

A human killing machine.

They might have felt scared, but at the same time they felt a sense of security. Iris looked like he could handle any situation now. The group of sorority girls that lived on the first floor called out his name as he walked past their door. He turned to see them all waving at him in their underwear. Any other time they would have dismissed him. Now they wanted him.

Especially because he did not want them back. Its human nature to want what you cannot have. Then once you get it the desire is all gone. Glass half empty. Glass half full.

The SUV engine purred with a silent but strong start. The duffle bag sat in the passenger seat under a jacket. Iris had placed one pistol between the center console and his seat. Never know when he would have to use it on the fly. He drove for hours.

The concrete roads and skyscrapers turned into dots then disappeared into the rear view. It was all forests and hills now. Peaceful scenery before a potential massacre. The calm before the storm.

The GPS showed the cabin was only a few hundred yards away. Iris pulled the SUV off into a wooded area so it would not be spotted by anyone coming up the road. Last thing he needed was to be flanked while doing his recon of the area. James suggested he should take the reigns on this one. Not arguing with the fact this could get him killed he obliged and let James take control.

Eyes closed then open. Immediately his stance changed to aggressive. His knees bent and shoulders pushed back to be ready for any fight. He reached into the duffle pulling out the kevlar and CQC modified M4A1. It had a recoil compensated stock, reflex sight, and a shortened barrel. He slung it over his shoulder. Clipped grenades to his vest. Put the ammo clips into their respective slots. Inserted the knives into their sheathes.

Finally, he took a M1911 out of the duffle. He inspected the guns sliding mechanism. Made sure it did not jam. He put one in the chamber then slid it into the pistol holster on his hip. Since Iris's face could put his family in danger it had to be covered. James put a face wrap over his mouth and nose. It was a black half face cover with a skull imprinted on the front. Go time.

James moved systematically through the woods to the front of the cabin. Doing visual sweeps of the area through the sight of his assault rifle. He moved so fluidly. Tactically. A veteran of many wars both foreign and domestic. As he approached the porch, he saw the door was slightly open. James switched the firing mode to full auto.

Lining the M4A1 with his shoulder he aimed down the sight. Slowly inching towards the door, he looked for any signs of forced entry. He pushed the door open slowly with his foot. It creaked open to reveal a room turned upside down. Papers were everywhere and furniture was flipped. Someone had been there looking for their target. He examined the room to find any sort of evidence on who had done this.

"Hey man over there by the fireplace" Iris said.

James walked over to see a still burning cigarette. He picked it up to exam it. It was a Dunhill cigarette. James kicked a chair across the room, and it shattered against the wall. The noise was loud and was followed by another softer sound. It was someone coughing.

James moved towards the bedroom and discovered his target strapped to a chair with jumper cables attached to his genitals. James had seen this technique before. The man was strapped to a chair gasping for air. He could not talk.

At a closer look he saw the man's tongue was gone. As he tried to unstrap the victim, he noticed something lodged in his chest. It was a giant syringe. The label on it was dated for the day the man had escaped the harvester. A note lay on the ground next to him.

"No one escapes" the note read.

James knew exactly who did this. The cigarette was his favorite brand. The technique of torture had his name all over it. The man in the chair was suffering. Dying slowly from what he had been put through. It was time that Iris learned a valuable life lesson. James closed his eyes. Iris was back in control.

"wait what are you doing?" Iris asked.

"the man is in pain give him peace" James replied.

Iris stood there in all this gear. Dressed like a true killer. A warrior. Yet when the time came, he could not take a life. He just stood there frozen. Sick to his stomach.

"the longer you wait the more he suffers" James explained.

Iris set down the rifle on the bed. Withdrew the pistol from its holster. He held up his arm and pointed at the mans head. The gun rattled as his hand shook. The man was suffering yes, but he could see into his eyes. The man didn't want to die, but he was going to either way. This was doing the humane thing. The right thing. Sometimes whats in someones best interest isn't what they want at all. He knew that better than anyone. Iris took a deep breathe. Closed his eyes. Counted down in his head.

five...

four...

three...

two...

one...

Iris squeezed the trigger, and a shot rang off. The man and the chair fell to the ground. He opened his eyes to see what he had done.

The wall was painted in blood and brain matter. The man lay lifeless and silent. Still strapped to the chair. His eyes closed. He must have accepted his fate at the last moment. Iris could not help but let out a tear.

It wasn't sadness or empathy. It was regret. He could never go back now. Iris walked out the cabin and made his way back to the SUV. He jumped in the front seat and started the engine.

Driving off down the road James tried to converse with Iris in his head, but it was no use. Iris completely turned off his thoughts. He was silent in both voice and mind. His eyes were finally open to how ugly the world really was.

CHAPTER 13-

He drove the vehicle down the dusty road. Looking past the scenery into nothing. Just a blank stare. His mind had shut down. Iris could not comprehend what he had just done. The feeling of squeezing the trigger mechanism. How easy it was for such a small action of a finger to end someone's life. The sweet but painful release of the pressure after the bullet left the chamber.

James did not try to speak to Iris anymore. He knew he needed time. Iris was just a kid compared to himself. He was not meant for this type of evil. Yet he had gotten tossed into it without any forewarning. Cosmic circumstances. The universe playing its giant game of chess. Always three moves ahead while we are six moves behind.

Iris's eyes were bone dry. His hands had quit shaking. He tried to convince himself it was necessary. It was warranted. Yet doubt lingered in his mind. The man in the chair was not a harvester. He was just another civilian casualty in this war of darkness and deceit.

His train of thought was interrupted by a piercing sound. The front windshield blew out and glass began to spray everywhere. Iris closed his eyes. James threw his arms up over his face and ducked below the steering wheel. Another shot rang off and the engine block was destroyed.

The SUV went off the road and rolled down into the woods. Once it had stopped rolling James unbuckled himself and grabbed the duffle. He slipped out through the front windshield and hid behind a pile of brush. Three men came into view at the top of the road. They were all wearing full tactical gear with ACR assault rifles. The men began to open fire on the SUV as they advanced down from the road. All three of the men had precise aim. Each of them targeting different exit points from the vehicle and shredding the doors with bullets.

James knew there had to be an overwatch somewhere. The rifles they were carrying were not strong enough to destroy the engine block with one shot. The caliber had to be .50 or higher. Armor piercing rounds. A bolt action of some sort. Inspecting the three men's gear to see if they had anything of use to him.

He spotted an earpiece on the one in the middle. That guy was to die first so he could not call for help.

James picked up a big rock and threw it at the back doors of the SUV. It made a loud enough noise that the men focused their fire on it. James ran out from behind the brush and started opening fire. Doing three round bursts to control the recoil.

He struck the man on the left in the chest and neck. Blood spewed out from behind the mans body armor. James had loaded his M4A1 with armor piercing rounds before the trip. The two remaining men took cover and returned fire in James's direction. Ducking behind a tree James unclipped a flash bang grenade from his vest and tossed into the SUV.

One man was blinded by the light and the other fell to the ground. James had aimed right. The grenade had landed in the vehicle and caused enough force upon detonation that glass and ammunition shrapnel flew everywhere. James dashed towards the men while he pulled out his pistol.

Before the blinded man could see an outline of James, he had already received a bullet to the head. The mans legs buckled and fell lifeless into the grass. A pool of crimson running from his face. James walked up and put another one into his head just to make sure.

He did not take chances anymore. The last man lay on the ground screaming in pain. The glass and bullets from the back of the SUV had sprayed all into legs. He clutched his legs trying to pull out the giant shards of glass. James knew it was no use. If the man removed the glass from its deep resting place, then blood would surge out and he'd bleed out in seconds. James walked up pointed a gun to his head and stepped on one of his legs. The man screamed even louder.

"Who is your fire team leader?" James demanded.

"Fuck you" the dying man replied.

James upset with answer put a bullet in each of the man's kneecaps. He was in so much pain that when he tried to scream no sound came out.

"I'll ask you again" James said.

"Fuck you i'm not telling you shit" the man spat blood at James.

Needing answers James decided to be a little harsher with his methods. He took out his knife and buried it into the mans leg right next to a shard of glass. He began moving it towards the glass causing it to tear up the insides of the mans legs. The man on the ground wiggled like a worm. His eyes rolling over from the pain.

"Stop i'll tell you whatever you want!" the man shouted out.

"Go on then" James smirked.

Right as the man was about to say a name a bullet ripped through his head. Brains and blood sprayed all over his Iris's face mask. James slung his rifle up and let out a barrage of bullets. Using his hip to steady the aim of the gun he ran to some cover. A fire fight began.

Bullets flew everywhere. They were slinging lead back and forth. The unknown assailant had to be the sniper who took out the SUV. His accuracy was almost perfect. The shots stopped for a moment. The man was reloading. James stood up to fire but was greeted with a round to his kevlar vest. He fell backwards. After his head hit the ground Iris was back in action. He had no idea what to do. Closing his eyes was not working for some reason. James could not be heard either. Something was up. Iris remembered his training and grabbed his rifle.

He threw a smoke grenade between them to get some distance. Just as he was about to fire a few shots into the smoke a man came flying through with his knee extended. It connected with Iris in his face and sent him flying backwards. His vision went dark for a second. He tried to stand but the man unleashed a barrage of kicks on his ribs and torso.

This was it. He was about to die.

The man grabbed Iris's head and began to twist. Iris grabbed a knife from his vest and stabbed it through the attackers hand. The man reared back in pain. He pulled the knife out and dropped it to the ground.

Before he could try to attack again Iris had his pistol pointed at the man. Without hesitation he pulled the trigger multiple times. His attacker fell to the ground. Iris walked over to him and shot him in the head.

It did not even phase him. His adrenaline was pumping. The pain from his beating had not set in yet. He searched the bodies to find a radio and a set of keys. Wandering up the hill beaten and broken he spotted the fire teams vehicle. The keys matched the vehicle make. Unlocking the doors, he set the duffle in it and closed the trunk. He got in the front seat and turned the vehicle on.

Putting it into drive he made his way away from the scene of rampage and wreckage. He was heading home. He needed to rest. To recover. His face was already starting to swell.

He could barely breathe. His ribs had to be broken. After that encounter he knew he needed to train even more. Somewhere where he was out of his element. To where he had to always be on alert. Always ready. He tried to speak to James about it and finally got through. The blow to his head must have cut off their communication for a bit.

"I wasn't ready." Iris spoke.

"Ive got a plan. We won't underestimate them again" James replied.

They ditched the vehicle a few miles from Iris's apartment and took a cab the rest of the way. Upon Arrival he began to look up some hot zones in the world that James had done contracts in. He explained to Iris he had some PMC contacts that he could call.

Say he was a mercenary looking for some work. Iris packed a bag with his passport and some clothes. They were on the next flight out of the country. Their destination was Central America. James knew some operators working there with the CIA and DEA to take down drug trafficking cartels. The harvester also had some production plants there.

Two birds one stone.

It would be the perfect real life training exercise for Iris. They were careless before and tried too early to carry out a mission. They knew their targets here would have to wait.

They would need to spend a few months in the fray fighting for their lives everyday. Get them ready for the enemy that lay ahead.

A bonus was the money from carrying out private contracts for the U.S. government always substantial. Iris was beginning to become a manifestation of James.

A killer. A soldier of fortune. A lost soul.

CHAPTER 14-

The plane touched down on a runway that consisted of dirt and dust. James figured it had been a makeshift location. Something for covert operations resupplies or non sanctioned extraditions. Iris stepped off the plane and was welcomed with humidity mixed with blazing sun rays. Was not the environment he was used to. He looked around to see some locals walking with mules and carts full of fruit. Iris noticed a man with sunglasses and a hat pulled over his head staring from afar.

"That's our guy" James explained.

Iris walked up and shook the mans hand. He was a brick house. A Spartan of a man with a battle-hardened expression on his face. The man led Iris to a convoy of covered trucks and jeeps mounted with .50 caliber machine guns.

These guys did not fuck around. Iris noticed the armed men inside of the vehicles were all different nationalities. Different flag patches placed on each of their own gear. Mercenaries.

Iris had heard about groups like this on the news when a private contractor and his squad opened fire on a civilian village in the middle east. Then again who really knows what happened. Sometimes freedom fighters and insurgents look just like everyone else. Knives and Stones in lieu of machine guns. After taking a good read of his new comrades he jumped into a jeep and introduced himself.

They all welcomed him with dirty jokes and bullying his smaller frame. The driver explained how he was from the states as well. Born and raised in the Midwest. Corn fed boy who went to war and found his calling. Traded his football scholarship for a tour of duty. Then after losing his entire squad and single handedly taking down a cell of insurgents he was offered a medal of honor.

Arriving home, he could not readjust.

All the noises gave him flashbacks of IED detonations and visions of his comrades losing their lives in that god forsaken desert. He was deemed unstable. A reject from the very society he had shed his blood to protect.

Desperate he reached out to a CIA contact he knew in the middle east who introduced him to Grey Sky Conflict Contracting. That was the GSCC Iris had spotted all over the gear of the mercenaries. Each man had their own origin story. They talked for hours as they drove behind the convoy. All the men kept their fingers on the triggers. Even the driver had a pistol in reach.

The area they were in was the perfect place to stage an ambush. Iris looked nervous. Even some of the operators he had befriended were on edge.

"I've got a bad feeling kid" James spoke.

"Me too dude" Iris replied.

It was too calm. No animals or people on the road. Just trees covering every inch of the skyline. The man in the passenger seat jerked his rifle to the right aiming towards a ridge line. The driver made a call on his radio to the rest of the convoy.

They began to slow down and come to a halt. It was so incredibly quiet. The only sound you could hear was the hiss from the truck engines cooling down. A branch broke and a figure came into view above the convoy on the ridge line. He was holding an RPG.

"Contact!" The driver yelled into his radio.

The man next to Iris let out a shot and time slowed down all around him. The rocket left its chamber right as the bullet struck its target. The rocket swiveled towards the convoy and struck the ground next to Iris's vehicle.

The jeep blew back onto its side from the impact of the rocket. Iris's vision went dark. He gained sight moments later only to realize the full extent of the attack.

After the rocket had fired multiple enemies emerged from the tree line and began firing.

The sound was deafening. Hundreds of bullets flew back and forth. More casualties on the opposing side than his own. The training showed.

Yet people still died right next to him. The man who fired the first shot was now pinned under the flaming wreckage of the jeep. Cut in half by the weight of the smoldering metal.

Iris walked over and closed the mans eyelids as he began to close his own.

James was back. He immediately picked up the nearest rifle and began laying down fire. Anyone he aimed at was dead shortly thereafter. His accuracy topped everyone else's on the convoy. Every shot he let loose met its target between the eyes or in the chest.

Not a bullet strayed from its path. James ran down to the next jeep and hopped into the mounted gun. Squeezing both the triggers the turret began to spin.

Bolts of fire flew from the multiple barrels of metal and shredded the landscape. Scores of men were cut into pieces when the giant rounds met their soft flesh. It became a massacre.

The remaining mercenaries flanked both sides of the enemy while James focused fire on the center. When the gun emplacement finally ran out of ammunition the remaining attackers all rushed to fire at James.

Before they could let a bullet out of their guns, they were surrounded by the GSCC forces. They all dropped to their knees and put their hands behind their heads.

Making his way up the hill James removed his sidearm and finished any wounded off. They would have done the same thing if the tables were turned. He made it to the top where the captives were being questioned. He inspected the men and their tattoos.

Most of them were all freedom fighters. Not cartel. James was very confused. They should not have been attacking this convoy if they knew they weren't cartel. Mercenaries and freedom fighters usually worked together here.

That is when he spotted the man with a familiar tattoo on his arm. James picked the man up and dragged him away from the group. The man shouted in a language he could not understand. Luckily, Iris could interpret.

He took control and asked the man about his tattoo. The man spat into Iris's face. Not a fan of that Iris struck the man in his mouth with the pistol. Blood leaked out of his gums and lips. Iris asked him again and the man began to tell what he knew.

He was only able to let out a few words when the GSCC forces opened fire on all the captives. Women and men were torn to pieces at point blank range by assault rifles. It was gruesome.

Even James was not okay with what was going on. The captives who did not die from the initial firing squad were greeted with bullets to the brain. The mercenaries took no prisoners.

They did not work within guidelines or laws. A job was a job regardless of who got in the way. The man Iris was questioning became horrified by the loss he just suffered. He screamed out "brother" in his own native tongue. Breaking free and filled with rage he pulled out a blade. Running with everything he had towards the mercenaries. He did not make it more than ten feet before he was gunned down.

Iris was hit with the blood spray. Something he had to become familiar with more and more everyday. He was appalled by the mass killing he just witnessed. The group of captives had to have been more than twenty-five strong. Ranging from all ages. The mercenaries began to dig a giant pit.

They dumped the bodies in it and set them on fire. One man grabbed a flag from his vest and smeared it with blood. Leaving it on the ground next to the mass grave. It had the cartel insignia on it. These men were committing war crimes and using the drug cartels as a scape goat.

"I had no idea corruption had gone this far" James spoke quietly.

The country was suffering from a genocide. Except this was not over religion or race. Ideologies were absent on this slaughter. It was all for money. All for greed.

The men walked up to Iris and began to thank him for his actions during the ambush. Iris nodded and told them it was no problem. He could not question their moves now or else he might end up in a ditch with a bullet in his head too.

He knew him and James would need to figure out what the fuck was going on down here. The man he had questioned only had one thing to say before he ran headfirst into death. The man said his soul was not safe. Iris could not figure out what he meant by that.

"The devil walks among us" A mercenary said under his breathe next to Iris.

A man that had been sitting comfortably in his jeep during the firefight had finally stepped out. He was wearing blue jeans with a white polo shirt. His chest was covered by a black Kevlar vest and his eyes were covered by even blacker sunglasses.

Iris figured this guy had to be calling the shots. He was clean cut. Looked like he had not seen battle in awhile. His face relaxed and smiling in this blood drenched landscape. He walked up casually to the mass grave and smirked. Spitting on the bodies in the fire.

"Waste of my fucking time" The man laughed.

The man in the sunglasses told the men to scavenge for any guns or ammo that had not been destroyed. They could be sold at the markets in the next town. Another way for them to make money. Kill the men and sell their guns back to the families looking for revenge. They would all meet the same fate. To take up arms against these men meant certain death.

To the outside eye Iris was just like them. He was there when they gunned down the people. He said nothing. Did not even look away. Part of him wanted to but the other part needed to see it. It was necessary to see how easily all those lives could end. To fight a beast, you must live and hunt like it.

Become so much like it that when you finally kill it you replace it. The unbroken cycle of murder.

The man with the sunglasses called over to Iris.

"Mighty fine work there son" The man said proudly.

Iris nodded and thanked him for the compliment. The man told Iris to walk with him for a bit while the men finished cleaning up the site. He asked Iris if he had been told what GSCC was doing here. Iris simply stated he did not care to ask because it was just another contract. The man in sunglasses liked his answer and smiled.

He began to tell Iris of their involvement. They had been hired by a pharmaceutical company to protect their interests in south America. It seems the locals had been upset with some of the experiments being conducted in their countries. Iris asked what happened to the cartels and the man replied with a simple answer.

"Money makes anyone an ally" He spoke.

The cartel was working with GSCC to keep production and delivery at a steady pace. Meaning the recent reports on civilian casualties due to drug cartel disputes were staged. Most of the innocents slaughtered were killed at the hands of an outside force.

Other countries had to have known about this, but if they were getting paid then what did they care about some farmers dying in the jungle. Profits over peace.

All the men assembled back at the convoy and loaded up. They made their way to a compound protected by military grade security measures.

This had to be one of the pharmaceutical companies' base of operations. The convoy rolled into the gates and the men started to head towards the barracks once they were out of the vehicles. It was getting dark. They had been driving for hours. Iris needed sleep. James needed time to plan.

After an hour or so of eating at the chow hall Iris made his way to his cot. He called this place home for weeks. Adjusting to the GSCC schedule and their way of life. Then one night they made their move.

"Get up kid. Time to do some digging" James whispered.

CHAPTER 15-

Iris slowly moved out from under the blanket and slipped his feet to the floor. Looking around for anyone watching while he snuck away from his cot. The barracks was silent besides a few grizzly men snoring away their day of battle. He made his way out to the camp and began to survey his surroundings.

There was a man patrolling the camp and occasionally checking in on his radio. Thirty-five feet up was a snipers nest on the roof of the chow hall. A man was stationed there looking out of his night vision scope toward the tree line. They were expecting something. Probably retaliation from the locals for the massacre that occurred.

"Timing is everything kid, watch for when the sniper moves his rifle to the other side of the nest" James explained.

Just as James had said the sniper began to move his rifle to be able to aim another direction. Once the barrel was lifted Iris made a run for it. He dashed through the dusty streets of the GSCC camp. Stopping every few moments to avoid being seen by a spotlight. As he ducked behind a bush, he saw men in lab coats walking with armed guards. They had to know something about was going on here. Iris tailed them around the camp until the men stopped at their private quarters. The lab workers proceeded inside, and the armed guards went back to their usual duties.

"You might have to get rough to get the info out of these guys" James spoke.

"After what i saw today i have no problem with that" Iris replied.

His face was stern. Blue and green eyes cold as ice. Iris waited outside the private quarters until the lights went off inside. Once it was pitch black, he crept in through a window. He was as silent as he was swift. Moments later he leaned over one of the beds that was occupied. A man lay there sleeping with no idea of the nightmare that loomed over him.

"Time to get up doctor" Iris whispered into his year.

The man shot up but before he could scream Iris already had a hand around his mouth. He pointed his pistol into his ribs to keep him quiet. The man was scared out of his mind and the room began to smell of urine. Iris told him to keep quiet and lead him to the laboratory.

The man did not want to die so he did as he was told. They made their way out of the private quarters and back onto the main paths of the camp. He led Iris to a passage hidden underneath a crate of armaments. The door was secured with both an ID reader and retinal scan. The man looked at Iris and was welcomed with a nod. He swiped his ID card and scanned his eye. The door made a soft beep and opened.

He watched as the scientist went down the ladder into the laboratory first. Iris looked around the camp one last time before heading down himself. The ladder went at least five hundred meters underground. Whatever was down here they were trying to keep it well hidden. The biggest secrets are always hidden deep from humanity. As he reached the last step on the ladder, he noticed his surroundings. White floors met with glass walls. You could see endlessly from room to room. Whoever designed it wanted to keep an eye on everything at once.

"Where's the main server room?" Iris asked.

"This isn't a data archive, its a collection facility" The scientist explained.

Iris noticed the glass rooms more clearly. In each one lay a multitude of beds. In those beds lay people hooked up to machines monitoring their vitals. Iris walked into one of the rooms to examine it.

"Stop you'll contaminate them" The scientist yelled as he chased after him.

Iris swung his fist out and connected with the mans jaw. He immediately went limp. Out cold. Iris stepped over him towards the bed. He pulled the blanket off revealing an elderly woman laying in a comatose state. She was breathing fine, but she was not there. Just a shell.

Nutrition was being pumped into her to keep the body alive. Iris began to pull more blankets off and saw the same result each time. Women and children were mainly amongst them. Iris was enraged by what he saw. He walked over to the man on the ground and picked him up.

"Wake the fuck up and tell me what's going on here" Iris yelled as he smacked the man in the mouth.

The scientist finally came to and began to explain what their mission was here. They were originally hired and brought here to produce a new drug for the American and European markets.

At first no one knew much about the drug or its origins. After awhile the scientist was granted clearance and learned it all. The extraction of life. The process of restructuring it. He thought he was breaking through to the other side of medicine. At first it was people on their death bed already on the way out.

Then it became something much more sinister. People started showing up in the lab who fit the description of missing locals. Then the forced experiments came. Trucks full of women and children arrived. All crying and scared.

Their husbands and fathers had been gunned down trying to protect them. That explained why there was barely any men in these beds. They had all either died when the GSCC forces came to collect, or they joined up in arms against these foreign invaders. They stood no chance.

"Our souls are not safe" Iris spoke.

The man at the mass grave said those exact words to him. This is what he meant. The people were taken from their homes and kept halfway alive to be drained. They were nothing but bodies now. Their souls diminished long ago.

"Why are they still here if their souls are gone?" Iris asked.

"Their life force can be replenished if kept alive" The doctor explained.

Iris was sick to his stomach. James began to anger on the inside. He yelled in Iris's mind and for once it was heard through another person's ears. Iris was astonished at what just happened. James had taken momentary control from his inner rage. Then out of nowhere Iris was sitting passenger in his own body again. His eyes never closed.

James had taken the wheel forcefully. He picked the scientist up and began to beat him senseless. Throwing the man around the room into beds and monitors. He hit James in the throat and tried to run.

He poked the bear.

As the doctor made his attempt to escape, he felt a searing pain in his leg. When he looked down, he saw a blade sticking in his thigh. He fell to the ground screaming in agony.

James walked over and stomped his foot down on the man's left kneecap. A loud crunch could be heard. The man began to seize up from all the pain. It was only the beginning. James picked the man up and held him face to face.

He looked at him before he removed the knife from the man's legs. He proceeded to stab the man repeatedly in the stomach and groin. With every push and pull of the blade the man's eyes lost a little bit of life.

"No motherfucker you aren't done yet" James shouted.

He dug around some drawers until he found what he was looking for. He popped the cap of the needle and stuck it into the mans chest. As he began to press down the man began to wake up and scream. James had shot him full of adrenaline.

He would stay awake for this new hell that was created just for him. James dragged the man over to an empty bed and strapped him in.

He found the extraction chamber underneath the bed and hooked it up. The scientist wriggled and screamed to be let go. It was no use.

The contraption began to lower a needle into the mans chest. It slowly drilled into his chest cavity and began to suck out a light blue substance. The face began to shrink into itself. Circles around his eyes began to darken.

At one point the man began to smile welcoming death. James unplugged the machine at the last moment. Leaving the man in suspended existence. Neither here nor in the after. He would be doomed to an eternity in this place. His personal purgatory.

James looked up to the ceiling almost as if the scientist's spirit lingered there. He pulled out his gun and shot three rounds into the mans head. His anger dissipated and Iris regained control.

Before they could talk about what just happened an explosion was heard above ground. The room shook a little and Iris ran towards a computer monitor he saw when he first entered.

He looked at the screen only to see an overwhelming rebel force storming the gates. Bullets flew everywhere as the GSCC men were slaughtered running from their barracks. The ones who did not wake were hacked to pieces by machetes while they lay in bed.

Karma is a real bitch and justice can be gruesome at times.

A smile crept across Iris's face before he was hit over the head and went unconscious. Two men threw a hood over his head and dragged him away farther into the lab. A third man followed behind them smoking a cigarette.

Whistling a tune as he initiated a self destruct sequence on a terminal. The two men dragged Iris onto an elevator while they waited for the smoking man. He flicked his cigarette onto the ground as he said his final goodbye to the lab.

"What a fucking waste" The man spoke softly.

He proceeded into the elevator and the doors shut. As the elevator arrow pointed up the room began to fill with gas. A small rumble was felt as they reached above ground. They dragged their captive out and sedated him before tossing him into a trunk.

The vehicle drove away from the camp as the night sky lit up from a massive explosion.

The jungle night roared with cries of agony that would go on unanswered.

CHAPTER 16-

Iris awoke to a bucket of ice-cold water being thrown into his face. He looked down to see he was tied to a chair. His hands behind his back and his ankles tied to the legs of the chair. Trying to break free proved to only anger his captors.

The two men took turns striking him in the stomach over and over. After a bit they switched to his face. Iris could feel each hit more than the last. They hit harder and harder every time.

Iris's vision grew blurry as he spat blood at the men. One of them proceeded to grab a blow torch off the table next to them.

"Hang in there kid I'll get us out of this" James assured him.

The man sparked the torch and turned up the flame. A blue phantom of heat met with Iris's chest. He screamed as the flame melted away the tattoos on his skin. It bubbled up different colors from the ink rising to the surface.

Iris was in excruciating pain. The two men took turns with the torch. Each time burning a different tattoo off his body. They laughed sadistically as they enjoyed every moment of their torture methods.

Iris tried to hold back his screams, but the feeling was too much to bare. One man leaned down to burn his arm, but the torch got too close to the wrist restraints.

After seeing it singe, he put the torch back. The two men talked amongst themselves as they grabbed a rag and a five-gallon container of water.

"Iris I know this is rough but no matter what they do you can't talk" James spoke to Iris.

There was no reply. After enduring such pain, he was in an altered state. The men pulled his head back and placed the rag on his face. They began to pour water onto his head.

He tried to gasp for air, but it was pointless. Each time he coughed the water up the rag just made it go right back down. He was drowning and started to lose consciousness just as they pulled the rag off.

"Who sent you here?" The man screamed into his face.

Iris said nothing so they hit him a few more times and put the rag back on his face. They dumped so much water on him James was astonished Iris had made it this long.

He was proud of him for being so tough, but every man has a breaking point. They just had to find Iris's. James looked around the room through his vessel's eyes trying to find some way out of this. Then he remembered the singed wrist restraint.

"Hey buddy i got this just close your eyes" James spoke.

"I can't close my eyes, i can't feel anything" Iris replied aloud.

The men laughed as they heard Iris mutter those words.

'You've got to try kid" James shouted.

Iris closed his eyes and James was there in an instant. He began to taunt the two men. Calling them pussies for water boarding instead of doing the tough stuff.

They grew raving mad after he dealt a blow to their pride. One man walked to the table of torture tools, and just like that James had his opening. He whispered something so the man left there would lean closer.

As the man lowered his head to listen James lunged forward and ripped his throat out with his teeth.

The man fell backwards clutching his throat as blood spewed from the wound. James spit flesh and esophagus out as he swayed the chair forward onto the ground. He looked into the mans fading eyes as he got his wrist free.

Grabbing his captors gun, he shot the man at the table in the head just as he had turned around.

James dug around for a knife and found one amongst the corpse with the missing throat. He cut himself free and staggered towards the torture table. He threw on the mans jacket and grabbed a set of car keys out of his jacket.

James made his way out of the room and down the hallway. He had to use the wall to support him. Iris's body still had not recovered from the shock. He looked down to see the young man's body covered in burns. Iris would be scarred forever. James felt an overwhelming amount of guilt for putting him through this. He finally made it outside to a vehicle. Another chance of life.

Right as he opened the door a shot rang off. James fell to the ground and looked around for his attacker. He could not believe what he was seeing.

Right in front of him was the great betrayer. Cooper walked up holding a pistol in one hand and a cigarette in the other. He pointed the gun at the ground next to James and let a shot off in the dirt.

"You've got some skills kid I'll give you that" Cooper said as he took a drag of his cigarette.

He flicked it away before adding a kick to Iris's ribcage.

"You're still a grunt compared to me" Cooper spoke again.

He began to beat on Iris. Applying pressure on his burns to cause more pain than his fists could deliver.

James could not feel Iris's pain, but he knew in his mind that the kid was suffering. James swung around kicking Cooper's legs out from under him. He lunged himself onto his feet as his nemesis fell to the ground. Cooper looked up astonished after being bested.

His rage grew and he flew at James with a barrage of strikes. The two men exchanged blocks and blows for what seemed like minutes. Each of them countering the other.

James could tell Iris's body was beginning to run out of strength. Cooper took advantage by grappling him to the ground.

He managed to get his arms around Iris's neck and started to choke him out. Just as James could see things getting blurry the tightness stopped. He could breathe.

Cooper let go and stood up. James turned around to see that his attacker was being held at gun point.

An old woman had picked up Cooper's pistol and aimed it at him.

"Big mistake grandma" Cooper exclaimed with a grin on his face.

"This is between us coop" James spoke.

A look of confusion swept across Cooper's face. He could not figure out how this kid would know his name let alone his nickname.

The fighting style reminded him of James but that was impossible.

"Go my child" The old lady spoke.

James stood up and got into the vehicle. He started the engine and drove away from the village he had ended up in. The sun began to rise as he gained distance from Cooper.

In the rear view he see could men surrounding the old woman who had helped him escape. She dropped the pistol and they put her on her knees. Cooper grabbed a knife from his waist and looked towards the vehicle as he cut her throat open.

Their eyes met in the rear-view mirror as the ground turned red at Cooper's feet.

After days of driving through the jungle and countryside James found a small clinic. He got patched up as best as he could given the circumstances. He procured a flight out of the country with some cash he had taken from his captors.

The pilot hid him amongst some smuggled cargo. He needed to get Iris to a real doctor before these wounds became infected and killed him. James remembered Red from Iris's apartment. That guy was their last chance.

CHAPTER 17-

The rickety plane touched down on a private airstrip outside of the city James used to call home. It would never look the same after he saw its undead counterpart. The skies were emerald, green on this particularly beautiful day, but all he could see was swirling grey clouds. A constant reminder of his misfortunes and self-inflicted damnation. Iris lay dormant in his mind and there was no bringing him back for now.

James needed to get back to the apartment as quickly as possible. He hailed a taxi and gave him the destination. The taxi driver could not help but look concerned for his passenger.

James was losing consciousness while Iris's body began to seize up from the burns. They arrived minutes later, and James paid the man before falling out of the cab. He proceeded through the front doors past the mailbox and stumbled up the stairs.

His hands shook as he inserted the key into the lock. Falling through the open doorway he walked toward the bathroom. Struggling to turn on the light switch he began to see the extent of damage done to Iris's body. He would never look the same.

"Hey kid can you hear me in there?" James asked.

Still no reply. The only thought that came to mind was getting him the help he direly needed. He would have to tell the doctor what is really going on if he could not get Iris to come back.

James shuffled Iris's broken body towards the bedroom to find the kids phone. Rummaging through drawers he stumbled across it buried under rolling papers and a folded-up picture.

James unfolded the picture and wept. A tremendous wave of guilt swept over his cold broken soul. There were things Iris still did not understand. Still did not know. Things he could not comprehend right now. So, James put the picture away and buried the thoughts and truths away deep.

Scrolling through the phone he found Red's number and sent him a message.

"911. Injured bad. Need help"

He figured that would get the point across. So now he had to play the waiting game. Looking through old albums and drawings he began to understand Iris more. He found his poems which were actually good. Incredibly sad, but good, nonetheless.

The kid was not cut out for this. Unfortunately, this was just the beginning too.

CHAPTER 18-

Iris awoke to complete darkness. Confused and somewhat frightened of his surroundings. He was trying to figure out if he was back in the void he had met James in.

Wondering what became of James and his own body for that matter. Trying to reach out but with no prevail.

He began to walk the darkness till he felt water on his feet. He looked down to see a small brook filled with black pebbles. The water on his skin made him feel alive and comforted in this desolate place. The best course of action was to follow the water and so he did.

After what seemed like hours the brook opened to a river. At the mouth of the river was a dock. Sitting on that dock was a mysterious figure.

The man on the dock skipped rocks across the water and sang songs to himself in an old language Iris could not understand. As he was walking, he stepped on a stick making a loud crunch. The figure turned to look at Iris and revealed a skeletal face.

"Hello, my old friend" the skeleton spoke.

"Do I know you?" Iris replied.

The skeleton motioned to him to sit next to him on the docks. Iris obliged and took a seat. There was a long silence, but something seemed so familiar to Iris about this colossus of what was once a man.

"So how do you know me?" Iris inquired.

"It's a fucked-up world we live in Iris" the skeleton replied.

Then like that it clicked. Iris stood up and hurried backwards.

"You're the guy who gave me the stem" he exclaimed.

The Skeleton nodded in agreement and began to speak his true purpose. It both reassured Iris and made him feel regretful of his choice to become part of this journey. The skeleton stood up and towered over Iris.

He said it was time they go and show Iris what remains unseen.

Both human and colossus walked side by side through purgatory as they made their way to an old cathedral and hospital far off in the distance.

As they finally got up to the door Iris was greeted by a man covered in bandages.

"Welcome chosen one" he wheezed through his beak mask.

They entered the hospital slowly as the sky rumbled in purgatory.

"The creator and the destroyer are beginning to lose grip with this place" The Skeleton spoke

"What do you mean by that?" Iris asked.

"Heaven oversees earth. Hell oversees the realm of torture. This Is the in between." He replied to Iris.

Iris began to understand where he was.

"So, am I dead?" Iris asked alarmed.

The doctor shook his head no and laughed. Before the Skeleton could reply

"You are here to see what must be seen and feel pain that must be felt" the doctor recited as he coughed out clouds of grayish lavender dust.

Iris was not worried. He did not feel emotional pain in his life besides the moment he mercy killed the man in the chair.

That was more regret than sorrow anyway. He felt confident he could handle whatever purgatory had ready for him.

He had no idea the suffering that would ensue.

CHAPTER 19-

The corridors of hospital were decaying and covered in illegible writings. The smell of death and lavender lingered so heavily that Iris had to cover his nose. Every step they took led further into the darkness.

At the very end there was a glowing light emitting from underneath a door. The doctor pushed it open, and a candle lit library was revealed. Towers of shelves filled with books occupied Iris's view. The doctor motioned him inside and closed the door behind him.

"What is this place?" Iris asked.

"Charon you can answer this one" the doctor replied.

The Skeleton who had remained mostly quiet in the hospital began to speak of man and myth. The time before and the time after.

How we only perceive things in a linear way and that is not how the afterlife works. The Skeleton somehow grew a sad expression over his boney face.

"I was born in a different time. Of a different womb." Charon stated.

"What do you mean?" Iris asked.

Charon walked over to a bookshelf and found an old tome. He dusted it off and handed it to Iris.

The book detailed the accounts of the Nephilim on earth and through history. Half angel half human. Some called them demigods back in the day of ancient Greece.

"I was once revered as blessing to mankind. People adored me and I treated them like peasants. I fought countless battles and death could never defeat me. I stood next to Achilles and Ajax. Then I watched them die all the same" Charon stated with sorrow in his voice

"Then how did you end up here?" Iris asked.

"I fell in love with a human. She made me forget about all the battles. All the bloodshed and loss. I felt equal to her. She did not see me as a god. She saw me as a human with a gift. Then the underworld swallowed her whole". Charon said remorsefully.

Charon spoke his heartbreaking story of how he searched for years through hell and purgatory to find her. When he finally found her, she was just another soul on the river Styx.

So, he made a deal.

He traded places with the ferryman so he could navigate the waters of eternity with her forever. So, he would never let her feel alone. Because she would never move onto the afterlife.

Her heart was on earth with him, and her soul stranded here.

Iris felt empathy for this divine stranger in front of him. As Charon closed the book on Nephilim Iris noticed a trail of tears down the skeleton's face.

"Even in death the heart still aches for what used to be" The doctor interrupted.

Charon shifted his tone to strong and confident. Masking his sorrow. He led Iris to a certain section of the library where it was chained up. The gate had a lock in the shape of an eye.

"who's going to explain to me what the fuck this eye is" Iris asked.

"It's the eye of Ra, goddess of wrath" Charon replied.

"In all religions there is one supreme being above all others. Some of you call it god, in my day it was Zeus, Odin, Ra. some call it Gaia. It has no form. It is a mother and a father. It loves us all the same." The Doctor mumbled

"Ra was the god of sun in Egyptian beliefs" Charon added.

"So, they eye of Ra is the force of balance. The unwavering hand of justice for the ultimate.

In your religions they call him Michael. Gods right hand." The doctor said before digging through more books.

Charon stood next to Iris and put a hand on his shoulder.

"The eye stands for the ones who will correct these injustices done to people's souls" Charon spoke.

"So, what does this have to do with me?" Iris asked.

The doctor moved over to Iris with an old scroll. It foretold of a time when man would cross the lines between life and death. Upsetting the balance and tearing the very fabric that holds all four realms separate.

"You are the one who will keep heaven and hell from colliding with earth." The doctor spoke.

Iris could not believe what he was hearing.

"why me?" he asked.

"The prophecy speaks of a child born with no heart. In your case that is your lack of emotions. Even your birth names origins are for an eye. You are the new hand of justice and vengeance Iris." Charon stated.

The doctor walked up to iris and pressed a gold coin against his head. Everything went white and the void was gone. He was sitting in his apartment looking in the mirror at his wounds and scars.

"Glad to have you back kid" James stated.

CHAPTER 20-

Iris stared at the wall of his apartment for ten minutes without blinking an eye. He could not grasp the concept of what he had just seen. What he was just told. He thought he was just a pawn in this war of souls. Only to find out he was the key to ending it all from the beginning.

"The unwavering hand of justice and vengeance" Iris spoke aloud.

He stood up and walked to the bathroom to look at his disfigurement once more. His chest had become charred and rotted. He needed help bad. Just as he was about to walk himself to the hospital there was a knock at the door.

"Hey Iris let me in bro" red exclaimed.

As the door was opening red already had started checking Iris's vitals.

"What the fuck man. You disappeared for three months and come back looking like a POW." Red said concerned.

"Its been a few hard months brother" Iris replied.

The doctor sat him down and began to check the severity of his wounds. Red looked concerned at the extent of the infections.

"Look Iris, I'm going to have to sterilize these wounds. Then I'm going to have to scrub the dead flesh off before it spreads." Red exclaimed

Iris nodded in agreement and took his shirt off. His tattoos were covered in burns and bruises. All the physical training he went through could not prepare him for the torture he endured. The thought of the torch against his chest caused a white-hot pain in his mind.

"Ready?" Red asked

The doctor began to pour peroxide and scrub off dead flesh. Looking up he expected Iris to be rearing back in pain. Yet he just sat there staring. Numb to the chemical burn he should be feeling at this moment.

Red wondered what had happened to the kid. He used to be a kind soul. Now a beaten warrior sat in front of him.

Hours passed as Red bandaged up Iris's broken body. He was mummified in gauze and aloe rags. They both knew he would never look the same. Iris accepted that fact. His mind focused on the task at hand.

The destiny he was assigned.

CHAPTER 21-

Iris tried to sleep; James even stayed quiet so the kid could reflect on his thoughts. Think about the pain and suffering he had been through. Or maybe think about the destiny he had been given. He felt so worthless his whole life, then just like that this cosmic game of chess chooses him as the key piece.

Every time he thought about the cabin his eyes focused on the wall. He would close them, and when they opened a mural of blood would be splattered across his view.

He began to realize the violence never goes away. It is a track stuck on a loop. Replaying the blood and feeling of taking a life over and over.

Tired of feeling stuck he gained his strength and got dressed. Pulling the shirt and hoodie over his burnt skin was painful.

Yet it reminded him of his mistakes, how he was too confident in his skills. Cooper had almost ended his life if it was not for that old woman in the village. She lost her life because of Iris.

"Why did you have to intervene" he said aloud to himself.

A solitary tear rolled down his face. Having another's soul in his body for so long was starting to give him emotions. Iris longed for that, but now the timing could not be worse.

Developing a heart just to put it through torture. He wiped his cheek and stared out into the city. He needed a distraction. Rummaging through his old phone he found her number. Natasha.

He had nothing to lose and everything to gain. Sure, he had James there, but Iris longed for another's affection. Especially since all the senseless loss of life he had become accustomed to.

The phone rang a few times then a soft toned woman answered. Iris exchanged pleasantries with her and proceeded to ask her out. She said yes. He began to clean himself up the best he could. Covering his bandages with long clothing. He had shrapnel scars on parts of his neck and face. He figured he would just say it was a car accident and leave it at that.

Two hours later Iris arrived at a nice restaurant near the harbor, he walked in and grabbed a table for two. Scanning the entries and exits he looked for any potential threats. An assassin first and a hopeless romantic second.

She walked in like sun breaking through dark stormy skies, her presence lit up the whole room. He stared in awe. She saw him and a look on concern swept over her face.

"What happened to you sweet boy?" Natasha asked with a heavy accent.

Iris sat her down and told her piles of lies. He felt bad he could never tell her the truth. The darkness inside him would only consume her. Ultimately destroy her. That made him reconsider the whole date.

"I should go I'm not good for you" Iris said as he stood up to leave.

"I can decide what's good for me on my own" she reassured him.

Natasha put her hand on his arm, and he felt at ease for the first time in months. The storm brewing inside was calmed. He saw the depths of purgatory, but her effect on him he could not explain. Sorcery of the heart.

Her smile and eyes put him at ease, Iris did not even think of the mission or the violence the entire time they were together. It was beautiful. It was perfect to him. He longed for his other half but never knew if she existed.

After hours of conversation and drinks Iris hailed her a cab. She asked if he would go home with her and he said yes.

The evening was spent with them connecting with one another on a physical and emotional level. She saw his wounds and scars. Yet did not judge.

Did not even ask where they came from. She just wanted him, and he just wanted her. Sometimes love can be as simple as that. Natasha fell asleep on his chest.

Iris stared at her ceiling listening to her breathing on his chest. He did not sleep. He spent every moment appreciating this little moment of light and warmth in his darkness. The morning came faster than he liked.

He got up slowly and let her transition gracefully to where he was laying. She looked beautiful and so peaceful sleeping. He did not deserve her. Not now after what he had become.

Iris left her a note and jotted a quick poem down. Setting it on the counter he walked out with his head held high. A smile grew across his battle weathered face.

On his way out he noticed a few black SUVs parked amongst the street. He thought nothing of it. He was at peace right now.

"Sir target located" a man with shades spoke into an earpiece.

As Iris walked home the convoy of black SUVs followed him.

"Kid you've got a tail" James spoke for the first time in days.

Iris looked back to see three black vehicles following his every move. The windows were too tinted to see how many hostiles in each.

"What piece do you have on you?" James asked.

Iris reached into his back waist holster and pulled back a .45 USP. Turning the safety off and putting one into the chamber. He was ready. The SUVs sped up and swarmed around Iris in the street. The first window rolled down and a silencer poked out. Iris let off two shots at the gunmen. The window shattered and the passenger fell back. Inside each SUV was a full team.

"Fucking run Iris" James yelled

He took off down in an alley climbing over fences as bullets flew by him. The teams broke off into a smaller groups to ambush Iris. A thought came to his head and he ran towards the water. Bullets flew everywhere, one striking an innocent bystander. He was dead on contact. Another meaningless casualty in the genocide of souls.

Smelling the dead fish in the air he knew he was almost there. Making a few sharp turns around street stands he lost the team amongst the fishermen. Iris slipped into a warehouse and hid. The armed assailants were outside asking questions. One man pointed towards the warehouse.

The teams reassembled and made their way towards Iris. Right as he was about to give up hope he heard a voice.

"It seems an old friend needs help" a man laughed behind Iris.

The man in the white suit stood there with a grin of confidence on his face. He extended a hand to Iris and they greeted each other. Iris explained his situation. The dragon head offered him a deal. His safety right now for a favor down the road. With no other options he accepted.

Flashbangs and smoke grenades flew through the windows as men adorned with black body armor swarmed the building. Once it had all cleared Iris stood there in the middle smiling. The men aimed there guns at him.

Right before the leader gave the command to fire, he looked up to see thirty plus men armed above them. Surrounded by gangsters. Outgunned and outmanned. He hesitated. That was the last thing he did. The man in white gave the order and his men rained bullets down on the teams.

Blood, bullets, and black body armor laid scattered on the floor. Iris walked up to the leader and took off his goggles. Attached was a video feed. Iris stared into it.

"I'm coming for you cooper" James spoke through Iris's mouth.

The video feed cut out. Behind the screen displaying it was Cooper and Alfred Mason.

"It seems we have a problem you chose to hide from me" Alfred spoke

Cooper looked down with disgrace. Anger and hatred in his voice he spoke up.

"I'll handle it sir" Cooper stated.

He sent a text to another team.

-Take the girl-

A group of men in a fourth black SUV emerged and headed into Natasha's building.

CHAPTER 22-

Iris said his goodbyes to the leader of the golden dragons. Stepping over bodies as he made his way out of the warehouse. The smell of death, gunpowder, and fish filled the air. He opened the door to leave looking up at his new friend.

"Don't forget you owe me now Iris" The man in white shouted.

That was a debt Iris did not look forward to paying back. Desperate times call for desperate measures. Taking one last glance at the scene of gore. Reminding himself how serious the threat he faced was.

The team of assassins sent after him lay slaughtered on the ground. The gangsters looting their corpses like spoils of war. He cleared his head and started to walk away from the harbor.

"I've had some friends dig up a few more harvester cell locations to take down" James stated.

"Then let's get to work" Iris replied.

He eventually made his way back home. Looking for any sign of forced entry before proceeding inside. Iris sat on the couch and laid his head back. Staring at the ceilings he had become so accustomed to. Murals of gray. Complimenting his cold heart.

"I know you have a lot to process kid, but I need a favor" James spoke.

"yeah, sure man anything" Iris replied confidently.

"I need you to go check on my family" James said with a sorrowful tone.

"Of course, brother" Iris assured him

Iris went to sleep hoping he could rest his weary bones. Thoughts kept his mind running at full speed the entire night. The gray murals became screens. His mind projecting the horrors and immeasurable loss. Adding PTSD to his long list of mental obstacles.

A loud bang outside caused Iris to roll out of bed. Grabbing a pistol from the nightstand he ran to the window.

Looking down outside he noticed a man limping away from a few shady individuals. After analyzing closely, he saw the man was bleeding. The men holding guns.

"Its not your fight Iris" James spoke

"Neither was the one with the harvesters" Iris replied.

He grabbed a mahogany bat from the side of the fireplace. Going to the kitchen he picked up a few steak knives. He dragged the bat behind him as he made his way to the ground floor of the apartments at three a.m., the entry doors opened with the sound of the bat dragging behind.

The man who was running fell to the ground. Begging for his life as the thugs pointed their guns at him. Laughing sadistically as the fear poured out of the man. The sound of knocking could be heard growing closer. The men looked around to find the source.

As the sound grew closer the men fired in different directions. Claiming their street gang lineage to instill fear. Yet the sound grew closer. The knocking became louder and louder.

The man bleeding on the ground looked over to see a dark figure dragging a bat behind him down the concrete steps. Every step he took the bat dragged and the knocking became deafening.

One of the thugs aimed his gun at the man with the bat. Before his finger could pull the trigger, a knife flew into his hand.

He screamed in pain before another blade connected with his throat. The other thugs fired at the knife wielding man as he took cover.

The moment they reloaded the unknown man vaulted over a concrete planter and threw two more knives into the group. Blood sprayed on the living as the dead fell lifeless accepting their fate by blade. Two left they tried to take on their attacker.

A blur of mahogany filled one mans vision before his skull split open and ended his life. Covered in his friend's brain matter the last thug fell to his knees begging for mercy.

He was greeted with a two swings to his knees.

Walking over to the victim he had just saved Iris extended a hand.

"Who are you?" the bleeding victim asked.

"I am vengeance" Iris replied simply.

He helped the victim up and handed him the bat.

"Finish what they started" Iris spoke.

The man obliged and grabbed the bat. Iris walked past the man with the broken legs on the ground. He bent down to whisper in his ear.

"Those who seek to harm will pay the price" Iris spoke as he stared into the broken man's eyes.

He walked up towards the front door of his building. Shutting the door behind him. In the background through the glass the once victim ended his attackers life with a barrage of swings to his body.

"Life or death" Iris spoke to himself.

CHAPTER 23-

Nightmares woke Iris from his sleep. The sound of police sirens could be heard outside. Officers and EMT's cleaning up his mess from earlier.

The concept of death was nothing to him now. Like breathing air. Once you are desensitized to it then nothing churns the stomach. Your demeanor like stone.

Getting out of he bed he walked to the fridge and took out his usual food. The same routine. The same food. The same violence.

Iris and James had become one in more ways than just sharing a vessel. Iris looked down at the plate as he cut the eggs with his combat knife. The yolks running gave him flashbacks of the cabin. His so-called mercy kill.

Blood and gore left Iris numb to death, but deep inside he felt regret for the innocents harmed on his path to fulfill the predestined. He swallowed down his thoughts of regret with the last swig of black coffee.

Bitter taste and bitter emotion compliment each other on the pallet.

"Before we head to the next target, I need you to go check on my wife and kid" James spoke.

"Let's go then" Iris replied.

The drive to James's house was silent. Neither of them spoke. Not through the mouth or the mind. Complete quiet both body and soul.

Iris reflecting on his fall into darkness. James nervous and heartbroken to see his family again under these circumstances. In the distance a glass and wood structure became visible.

"Home" James muttered to himself.

Iris pulled up slowly to the house. Kicking up gravel and dust on the solitary road. Appreciating the simplicity of it all he began to walk towards James house.

As he rang the doorbell you could hear a little girls laughter. The door swung open to a beautiful brunette with autumn eyes.

"Can I help you?" the radiant woman asked.

There was a pause with no answer. James was in awe. The love of his life and mother of his child stood right in front of him.

He had lost her and wandered alone for what seemed like an eternity. His bullet ridden heart shattering into cold dark dust.

"Hi mam my names Iris, I served with your husband" Iris spoke up.

The woman smiled and opened the door motioning him inside. Walking in memories began to fire off in their combined conscious.

Years of love and affection filled their vision. Iris stood there awkwardly staring at the interior as his mind was on auto pilot.

"My husband built this place" the woman spoke to break the silence.

Iris snapped back to reality and replied.

"James was a good man" Iris spoke.

He looked over to see a tear running down her face. He walked over and hugged her offering condolences. The embrace sent a shockwave through James soul. Iris backed away to end his pain inside.

"Sorry I'm just still getting used to him being gone" she spoke.

James watched his soul mate walk around and converse with Iris. Staying quiet for fear he would say something only he would know. Adding more to her plate.

She needed to move on and knowing his soul was wandering lost forever would crush her.

A little girl came running up to Iris and asked If he wanted to play. He shook his head yes and picked up her toys with her. Iris closed his eyes.

Sitting down listening to his little girl speak. James was so happy to see she was staying strong. They both were. His wife was his rock. She needed to stay that way for their daughter. He stood up and walked over to the stairs. Petting his dog.

"Close and comfortable" James spoke to himself.

He looked out to see a trail of dust coming down the gravel road. As it grew closer James filled with rage. The dust settled as an engine turned off. Both Iris and James went into defensive mode. Looking for the nearest weapon.

The front door opened. The guest was greeted with a hug and smile.

"Hey, we have a guest, one of your and James's buddies from the service" James wife spoke.

As Iris made his way to the backdoor to leave, he was greeted by a familiar grin.

"Been a long-time kid" Cooper said aggressively.

The tension was sucking the oxygen out of the room. The air filled with silent particles of revenge.

"Let's sit down for coffee and catch up" the wife spoke.

Cooper and Iris moved towards the dining room table. Watching each others every move. Sitting across from one another. Never breaking eye contact.

They sat down and sipped coffee quietly. Looking up to analyze the other. Mortal enemies on peaceful ground. All three of them knew not to let the violence come here.

"So central America right, that's where we served together" Cooper spoke.

He grinned waiting for a reply from Iris. Underneath the table were two pistols. Each one pointed at the other. Both Cooper and Iris ready for the other to make a move.

CHAPTER 24-

Cooper stared at his mysterious foe. Wondering how he was in central America, and now how he was in James's house. This young punk never did tours of war with him and James. Yet his fighting style mimicked James's in every way. He wondered if James had a pupil that no one knew about.

"Who the fuck are you?" Cooper whispered across the table.

"Vengeance" Iris replied simply.

Cooper laughed.

"You think that shit will scare me kid?" Cooper asked.

"It's the truth" Iris spoke.

Cooper was puzzled by this kid. Usually, people cowered in fear from him. Ran from his very presence. Now this unknown stranger sat staring back into his own lifeless eyes. No fear or hesitation.

"You fucked up kid. You have no idea who you pissed off" Cooper exclaimed.

"The harvesters time has come" Iris replied with anger in his voice.

Cooper stood up quick. The chair flying backwards behind and crashing into the wall.

"Everything okay?" the wife spoke from the other room.

"Yes, sorry got up a little too fast el" cooper replied.

James screamed inside Iris's mind. Thrown into a rage that Cooper called his wife by that name. The name he himself called her. The son of the bitch betrayed him, and now he sat in his home flirting with his wife. Playing house with the family he had robbed him of.

"Iris let me take over" James spoke in his mind.

As soon as their eyes opened James lunged at Cooper. Pinning him against the wall. He pointed his gun into Coopers ribs.

"I'm coming for the whole fucking network Cooper. One by one I will burn it all to the ground. Hunt you all to the ends of the earth, and the last thing you will all see before you die is me" James spoke

Cooper broke the hold and brushed himself off calmly.

"Not here kid. I wont bring the violence into their home" Cooper spoke.

He walked towards the door to leave. Waving goodbye to James's wife and daughter.

Iris eyes opened and he was back in control. He followed Cooper outside to his motorcycle. As he saw him get on the bike, he pointed his gun at him. They stared at each other. Cooper welcomed the bullet with his cold stare.

"He's right Iris. Can't do this here" James spoke.

Iris lowered his gun. Cooper kick started his motorcycle and drove away. The dust from the gravel separating sworn enemies. As he drove down the road cooper used his earpiece to call headquarters.

"Alfred it seems the kid knows about the entire network. Maybe a protégé of the order." Cooper said unsure.

"What aren't you telling me agent cooper?" Alfred replied.

Cooper hesitated.

"Agent?" Alfred exclaimed angrily.

"His training mirrors James sir" Cooper spoke finally.

On the other end of the call Alfred Mason stayed quiet. He picked up his phone and hung up on the call with Cooper. Smashing his fist into his desk. He walked out to a large glass wall. Staring out over the harvester site he helped build. He pressed a button under his desk and the glass wall turned jet black.

Walking over to his bookshelf he pulled out a book that turned out to be hollow. He opened it and took out a red phone. The cell only had one number in it. On the first ring the other end picked up.

"It has begun, the council must meet" Alfred spoke.

"Very well, we've been waiting a long time" a mysterious voice spoke.

Alfred walked to his computer and began typing in a series of numbers. A map of the known world opened. In each major city of the world a red dot appeared.

Locations of every harvester network. Phones rang in London, Beijing, Moscow, Sydney, and Tokyo.

With each call Alfred told them of the impending attacks. The harvesters were on red alert. Assembling their forces. Sending out spies and assassins.

They have been controlling the world behind the scenes for over a hundred years. They would not allow Iris to get in their way.

Doors slid open behind Alfred. Two men in combat armor walked in dragging a woman behind them. Her head covered with a black bag. She cried behind the cloth as she dragged her feet. The men sat her down in front of Alfred's desk.

He pulled off her hood. Revealing a blonde woman. One who was frightened and terrified.

"Who is the man that left your apartment this morning?" Alfred asked.

She looked up with false fear in her eyes. Natasha was waiting for this moment. Rearing up she connected her head into Alfred's nose and flipped behind her chair. She broke her zip tie restraints in half with one quick move. The two armored men rushed her.

One fell onto the ground screaming in pain as Natasha kicked his kneecap in. His weight buckling underneath him. The other attacker pulled a knife and slashed at her.

She turned it on him and stuck it into his neck. His life draining from his eyes while he choked on his own blood.

Natasha walked over to Alfred and threw him against his desk.

"What is the network planning you son of a bitch?" She screamed at him.

He spit out blood onto the floor laughing.

"The Order cannot stop what's to come" Alfred replied with bloodied teeth.

He lunged for underneath his desk. Grabbing a concealed pistol. Letting off shots at his female attacker. Natasha took one to the arm as she ran out the room.

Making her way to the exit elevator. Security swarmed behind her firing their guns. She slid into the opening elevator and pressed the close button.

Bullets ricocheted off the elevator doors as they closed. She took a deep breathe. Staring at Alfred in the distance before the doors fully shut. Traveling upward she made a call on her earpiece.

"They've started some sort of preparation; I couldn't find out what. They know about Iris" she spoke.

"Return to the sanctuary in Cairo." An agent of the order replied to her.

As the doors opened, she ran outside with blood running from her arm. She lost her pursuers in various alleys. Ripping her shirt and tying it around her bullet wound to stop the bleeding. On her arm an image showed adorned in a flow of crimson.

The eye of Ra.

Chapter 25-

Iris hugged James's wife goodbye. Let her know he would keep in touch. He went and said his farewells to the little girl. She smiled and hugged him as well.

Making his way out the house he could feel James suffering inside. Closing the front door behind him he took one last glance at his surroundings.

"I know that was probably very hard for you James" Iris spoke with empathy in his voice.

"That was the toughest thing I've ever done kid" James replied with sorrow behind his words.

They made their way back to the SUV they arrived in. Sitting in the front seat Iris contemplated on his own family. His past.

It had been years since he had come around. Once he stopped going to college, they were ashamed of him. Their name tarnished by his past choices and mistakes.

"You should go see them Iris" James spoke up.

"Not yet. Not till this is over" Iris replied.

He closed his eyes and inhaled deeply. Exhaling the guilt with each fleeting breath. Opening his eyes James was back in control.

"I need time to think" Iris spoke.

James started the engine and drove away from his family. Putting distance between himself and the ones who meant the most to him. An idea popped into his head of their next move.

Setting the GPS to his destination. A look of determination crept across Iris's face. It seemed the longer James was in control then the more Iris began to look like him. The vessel adapting to its controlling host.

In the back of their combined minds Iris sat in suspension. His conscious floating in a void of peace and quiet. The eye of the storm.

A storm made up of vengeance and sorrow. There Iris could look inside himself. In this corridor of his mind, he could be centered.

He sat there on the plains of consciousness meditating about his life. About the world he had been dragged into. Sometimes he thought about just locking himself away in this void. Letting James have another chance at life in his body.

That was not the prophecy though. Charon and the doctor told Iris it was him. It was always him. Since time immemorial. He took one last deep breath. On his exhale he shifted back into his body. His eyes opened and he was in control of the vessel once again.

"How did you just pull control from me?" James asked.

"Something I've just figured out I guess" Iris replied unsure himself.

"So where are we headed?" Iris asked changing the subject.

Before James could answer Iris already pulled up the GPS destination. A university showed up on the directions. The school Iris used to attend.

"Why are we going here?" Iris asked.

"That's one of the research labs for stem" James replied simply.

Iris was bewildered by the fact his old campus was conducting research on souls. His whole attendance there was plagued by a destiny he had not even realized yet. The prophecy seemed to have followed him. Small coincidences became a bigger picture. All of it worked up to this moment in time.

A few hours passed and they arrived at the University. It looked the same as when Iris had attended three years ago, and yet it felt off. Campus security was everywhere, and they had built entry check points into all the parking lots.

"What is this Guantanamo bay?" Iris spoke aloud.

They continued forward pulling through a check point. A man in a security uniform motioned them to roll the window down. Iris obliged.

"State your business" the security officer spoke.

"I used to go here. I'm trying to enroll again." Iris spoke quickly.

The security guard looked at him a few times. Checked out the vehicle he was driving and waved him through.

Iris pulled up to the visitor parking spots and turned the engine off. He took a deep breath. Readjusting his shirt collar and hair in the rearview. It had been so long since he had been here so he would not remember the layout.

"We need to get a campus guide" Iris spoke.

Looking to his right he saw a guide giving tours to potential students. Iris slowly made his way over to them. Slipping in the group while no one was looking. When the group finally made it to the science building, he split off.

"It should be in the chemistry lab that's closed year around" James spoke.

"how do you know that?" Iris asked.

"We had to know locations of labs in case they were ever compromised" James replied.

Iris made his way through the halls looking for a locked room. All the ones he could find had full classes in them. As he reached the back of the building, he finally found it. A door had hazmat tape on it with warning stickers. Using a chemical spill as a cover up to keep people out.

He cut the tape on the door with his knife. Slowly pressing open the door. As he entered, he only saw old lab equipment covered in dusty plastic tarps.

"I don't see anything man" Iris spoke.

"Its here somewhere" James assured him.

That is when they both noticed a faint light emitting from underneath a wall. Iris walked over and felt for a crease. Just as he put his hand against the wall, he heard a humming noise. He ducked behind one of the dusty tarps.

The wall split into two and elevator doors appeared. The doors opening to a scientist and his security detail.

"These people and their fucking secret elevators" Iris said with sarcasm.

The scientist noticed the tape on the door hanging down. He turned and pointed it out to his bodyguard. The bodyguard reached for his radio. His fingers never connecting with the button.

Iris sprung out and used a tarp as garrote. Choking the bodyguard till he fell limp on the ground. Iris yanked the plastic sideways snapping his neck. The scientist ran frantically to the exit. Right as got to it his sense of relief was met with a knife to his spine.

Walking over to the bleeding scientist Iris slipped on a pair of brass knuckles. Picking the knife, he threw out of his target. An exceptional throw. Right in the spine where it paralyzed his legs. Vengeance requires precision after all.

He dragged the scientist over to a chair. The man moaned in pain as Iris slumped his broken body into the chair. Getting picked up by his hair all he could see of his attacker was one green eye and one blue.

"I can't feel my legs" the scientist screamed.

"What's the code for the elevator?" Iris asked.

"If I tell you they'll kill my family" the frightened man spoke through bloodied teeth.

Iris did not like that answer. He pummeled the man's face over and over with the brass knuckles. The man became less recognizable with each punch. His face swelling from the damage.

"I'll ask once more" Iris said angrily.

The man had no response. Just fear and pain in his eyes. Iris lifted his hand to hit him again.

"retinal scan" The man cried out.

Iris grabbed him by the head and dragged him to the elevator. Placing his eye up to a small glass circle. The retinal scanner flashed red and denied him access.

"His face is too swollen kid; it can't read the whole eye" James spoke.

Looking down he understood what had to be done. Iris pulled out his knife and cut the scientist's eye out. He showed no mercy to anyone in the harvester network. They stole life itself, so pain and suffering was their price to pay for those unspeakable acts.

Placing the severed eye against the glass the scanner finally blinked green. The elevator doors closed on Iris. Inside he put together a machine gun that was disassembled in his backpack. Slowly he began sliding the parts into place. A loud click with each part connected.

The elevator hummed as it went down. The clicks became rhythmic. The hum in sync with the painful cries coming from the man at his feet. A melody of painful tones.

After restoring his gun and loading the bullets Iris put his tactical gear on. Sliding level four plates into his Kevlar vest. His pistol on his side. Blades fastened on his back. Pulling his mask over his face.

Iris had ditched the skull mask and came up with something to strike fear in his enemies. On his ballistic mask was an ironic depiction of revenge and justice.

A symbol that now resonated within him.

The elevator stopped. The ding chimed that signaled he had reached his destination.

A team of security guards waited guns pointed on the other side. The first thing they saw when the doors cracked open was a man dressed in dark black.

His face covered by a crimson red eye on a white mask.

The last image their eyes would see before the cold touch of death.

A living nightmare.

CHAPTER 26

Iris busted out the lights in the elevator before the doors opened. Two metal canisters bounced and rolled towards the guard's feet. A loud flash went off blinding everyone in the hallway. With swift movements he sprinted out the elevator laying down fire.

Controlled bursts made quick work of the front line. As some guards gave up hope and ran Iris gunned them down. The ones left alive on the ground he put down permanently.

As he made his way down the corridors of the lab, he left a trail of blood and suffering. Iris had become blood thirsty. His recent experiences taking away the last shreds of humanity he had. His mind scarred and traumatized just like his body.

"what are we looking for James?" Iris asked.

"It'll be a black door with three red circles" James replied.

Walking a few more minutes down the crimson-soaked floors he found the door. Entering the room, he was caught off guard. A chair connected with Iris's face and he fell backward. Springing up on his feet he rushed his attacker.

Grabbing the chair and throwing it across the room. It all happened so fast he barely had time to stop himself when he realized who had hit him. Iris's fist froze suspended in air.

"please don't hurt me" a young woman spoke with a frightened tone.

"Who are you?" Iris asked.

She looked up to see a tower of a man covered in black clothing with blood dripping from his hands and feet. His face obscured by a solitary eye. His face a twisted image that struck fear into her.

"I don't work for them I promise" the woman spoke quickly.

"Then what are you doing down here?" Iris replied.

"They took me to get to my dad" she spoke with a sad tone.

Iris took a closer look then it hit him all at once. Her eyes. Her cheeks. She was the daughter of the suffering man in the cabin. The offspring of his first kill. For one second his voice went weak.

"I knew your father." Iris spoke with regret.

The girl shook her head back and forth before breaking down into tears after hearing the way he had said "knew".

"What happened?" she asked.

Iris sat down next to her. Took off his mask. She could see the honesty in his eyes. Hear it in his voice. She knew her father was really gone. She fell against Iris's shoulder sobbing.

"You can't go home it's not safe. You can stay with us." Iris spoke.

"Us?" she replied.

He forgot no one else could hear or see James.

"Yea me and my doctor friend" he spoke unsure.

"Thank you so much" she spoke with some hope.

In his head James pondered on the implications this could have for everyone. A high value target taken from the harvester would bring a lot of search and destroy teams. But he could not help but think she would still have a father if not for him. So would his own daughter.

The decisions he made led him here after all.

They made their way out of the old chemistry lab, and back to the SUV. Leaving the campus, the woman fell asleep in the back seat. Iris covered her with his extra coat. One not covered in brain and blood. He occasionally looked in the rear view checking on his new friend.

She was the only other person in the world he knew who got pulled into this shadow war like he was. Iris felt a sense of connection to her. An even stronger sense of duty to protect her. After all she lost her father.

In his mind he replayed the scene over and over. The fear and pain in his eyes. The pressure of the trigger before the loud sound. Crimson canvas walls. He took a deep breath and floated away into consciousness.

James began driving the vehicle. One thing burning in his mind.

Cooper.

CHAPTER 27-

The wind flowed between his arms as he throttled his motorcycle home. Going so fast the images blurred. Mind racing from an earlier encounter. Confusion and regret lingering amongst horrors of the past.

A mind at war. A soul torn.

Everything he saw was analyzed. Potential threats. Emergency Exits. Constantly alert every minute of every hour. Some would call it madness. He called it Practice.

"Its all for the greater good" He assured himself.

Closing his eyes while swerving through traffic. Hoping for a sweet release. A quick impact to end his perpetual suffering. The screams echoed in his ears. Recalling every moment of every kill.

Trying to collect good memories, but there were none. Happiness absent from his upbringing. He lived by a code.

Nothing to lose. Nothing to fear.

He pulled up to his house and went inside. Wishing he had not made it back.

Cooper was a monster in his own right. Fangs disguised by a handsome face. Piercing blue eyes with no humanity behind them. Dead ocean eyes.

He had spent the past day trying to dig up intel on this new threat. A young adversary who mirrored Cooper's past mentor.

For a brief second you could see a look of sorrow on his face. Then just as fast it was gone.

"James why did you get in the way?" Cooper asked himself.

A text message sound disturbed his thoughts. Breaking away from his inner reflection he picked up the phone. The green bar showed an address. After writing it down Cooper took the sim card out and snapped it. Always disposing any trace of a job.

Cooper changed his clothes. Washed his face. Took a deep breath. Then he grabbed his keys to his truck. Walking into the garage he clicked the key fob. Lights on a solid black 1970s dodge truck clicked on. The engine roared.

Getting inside he threw into his reverse. Gently pulling out onto the street before flooring it. The smoke fumed from the exhaust. He reached for a headset. Placing into his ear.

"Four targets agent" a voice spoke from within the headset.

Speeding down the highway his grip tightened. With each exit he played different scenarios in his head. Any outcome. Any circumstance. He was ready.

Arriving at his destination Cooper flipped up his passenger seat revealing a compartment. Inside were foam inserts holding a variety of lethal weapons.

"Need something quiet and fast" Cooper thought aloud.

After rummaging through his mobile arms stash, he found it.

A KG9 submachine gun with a suppressor attached on the barrel. A folding stock clipped to the side.

Cooper tucked the gun into a holster under his jacket. It hung freely and blended with his clothes as he walked towards the door of the building.

The lights from the laundromat illuminated his face. A good front for what was really going on. As he walked inside a man from behind the counter told him they were closing.

Turning around Cooper began to lock the door behind him.

"What are you doing?" the man behind the counter asked.

Time froze for a moment before the laundromat clerk reached under the counter. Cooper dove behind a washing machine as bullets flew at him.

Returning fire from cover he pelted the clerk's chest killing him.

Cooper ran towards the door behind the desk. A camera caught a glimpse of him before he triggered a remote emp scrambler in his truck.

The whole store and block went dark. Cooper made his way down the stairs in the back. Walking lightly so no one could hear his footsteps.

In the distance panicked voices began yelling to one another. The sound of guns being cocked and loaded echoed in the basement of the laundromat.

Knowing he had only a few more minutes before the lights kicked on Cooper sprinted towards the voices.

"He's over here" One man shouted before cooper put a bullet in his head.

The dark corridors lit up in flashes. Shadows falling to the ground. Loud bangs followed by suppressed return fire. Soon it all stopped. Darkness loomed.

Cooper sat there a few minutes catching his breath. Waiting for the lights to kick on. Then all at once the darkness vanished. A room of white sprayed with red.

Blood-soaked sheets piled up in bins and on tables.

"The targets are eliminated" Cooper spoke to his handler.

"Burn all evidence. Extract any intel on his locations and allies." A voice replied.

Cooper found a laptop and ran a keyword search program. He typed a name in getting only one result.

He downloaded the file before triggering a system wipe.

After grabbing a gas can from his truck Cooper began dousing the laundry in fuel. Setting it aflame as he walked away from the inferno.

Wherever he went destruction followed. The monster of a man walked back to his truck with a mural of flames behind him.

Down in the basement the room began to crumble from the flames engulfing the supports. The laptop finished its system wipe as the fire reached the keyboard. The screen melting away revealing a burnt image.

A large Victorian home hidden amongst the cityscapes.

CHAPTER 28-

Iris stood at the doorway of a medical exam room. Red was inside doing a full check up on the girl he had saved. She was tortured. Frightened. Broken.

He remembered when had once felt that way. Flashbacks of his capture in south America triggered his PTSD. The sensation of his melting flesh coming in waves. The look of enjoyment in his captor's eyes as he screamed in agony.

"She's a tough kid Iris" James spoke within their unified mind.

Walking towards the foyer Iris looked at the ceiling of Red's historic home. The time it took to build. The detail. He drifted away for a second just on the concept of time. As he looked out the mosaic glass something caught his eye. A flash of light gleamed from the park across the street.

"Get down!" James shouted into Iris's mind.

Right as Iris ducked, a bullet pierced through the glass and hit the wall where he was standing. He crawled across the floor as more shots rang out. Glass flying in every direction.

"Red get her out of here" Iris screamed.

The butler tried to run across the foyer to cover but caught a round to the ribs. He slumped against the staircase. Looking up at Iris with fading eyes. His breathing slowed. Then he was gone.

Iris laid there staring into the dead old man's eyes. Another innocent gone because of him. His train of thought broke as he heard the girls scream.

"They're coming in through the back!" Red shouted to Iris.

The door to the patio busted open. A team of black armor-clad operatives stormed in. The leader holding a sledgehammer with a shotgun swinging from his shoulder.

"Breach and clear every room" The ops leader spoke to his men.

Footsteps stormed up from the backside of the house towards the foyer. Iris jumped up and ran towards Red.

"Where is your gun Red?" Iris asked.

Red pointed towards a safe under his office desk.

"The code is 420" Red told Iris.

No time to laugh. Iris sprinted towards the safe. Punched in the code revealing a colt m1911 with an extended clip.

Before he could ask why his friend had this mod on his pistol Iris ran back to the foyer. Right as he reached the top of the stairs the team was making their way up.

Firing shots as he ran back up Iris clipped an ops in the throat. The target slid down the stairs leaving a trail of blood.

"Focus fire. Pincer formation" The ops leader yelled.

Two ops team members ran up the stairs opposite of Iris to flank him. The other three pressed his forward position. Red grabbed two clear mysterious vials then disappeared down the hallway towards the flanking men.

"Red what the fuck are you doing?" Iris asked as he fired at his attackers.

"Just trust me" Red replied from down the hall before his voice faded.

The three-man team made it up to Iris. The first one swinging for his face but missed. Iris pistol whipped his attacker in the nose. Firing three shots into his chest as he fell backwards.

The man fell over the stair ledge. Landing on his neck.

For a moment, all three of them just stood there. The ops leader made the first move rushing into Iris and picking him off the ground. As he picked up Iris over his head the other member ran into the room to find the girl.

Right before the Leader could slam him down, Iris had wrapped his legs around his foes head and shoulders. With a strong twist both went tumbling towards the ground. Each of them stood up and exchanged blows.

Their movements like a dance. Iris countered the leaders every strike. In return the leader did the same.

"Let's see how the student matches up to his master" The leader spoke before removing his face covering.

The man pulled his ballistic mask off revealing his true face.

Cooper stood there with hatred burning in his eyes. He motioned Iris over to fight.

"This is my fight" James assured Iris.

James took over their shared vessel and charged at Cooper. Fists connected back and forth. Blood spewing from their mouths and face. Their battle of brute force raged on. So evenly matched. Almost like mirrored images.

"Give up kid you wont win this" Cooper said behind bloodied teeth.

James countered those words with a kick into Coopers knee. The pop it made was the satisfying sound James expected.

Cooper fell back gripping his leg. He tried to stand but his knee just gave out.

"Cheap trick" Cooper laughed.

As he walked towards Cooper laying there, he thought of all the good times. Their times in war. His brother in arms turned into his most hated enemy.

James pointed his gun at Cooper. His oldest friend staring back up at him.

"Close and Comfortable" James whispered into his ear before pulling the trigger.

Coopers eyes filled with confusion and wonder as the bullet entered his chest. His mind racing with scenarios. All his preparation had failed him. A part of him embraced the coming cold. Blood running from the sides of his mouth as he smiled.

"James" Cooper softly spoke between his labored breathes.

Pulling the trigger two more times James left three smoking holes in Coopers chest.

"Now we are even, rest in peace brother" James spoked aloud.

After hearing glass shatter, he ran into the room with the girl and the other attacker. The man in armor laid on the ground holding his stomach.

Acid burning through his armor and skin. The girl had thrown a bottle of chemicals at him to get away. Lucky for her it was the right chemical.

Iris regained control and walked over to the man with the melting torso. Putting a bullet in his head to keep him from suffering any longer. More sounds of glass and gun shots rang off down the hall.

Running to the other side of the house Iris found red holding his bloodied arm. One ops member was dead by his own hand. The other screaming in the corner.

"What the fuck happened to them?" Iris asked.

"Lethal doses of hallucinogens" Red replied slowly calming down from the firefight.

Broken vials were stuck to both ops members. A mysterious odor rising from their bodies.

"How long does this one have?" Iris asked.

"Two minutes give or take, before full psychosis like his friend here" Red responded.

Iris walked over to the man screaming from his hallucinations. A pillowcase was draped over the terrified ops member's head. Iris dragged him into a spare bedroom and shut the door. The small amount of light peeking through the pillowcase vanished.

The ops member screamed into the darkness. His mind collapsing. Reality was gone. He heard terrifying noises and pissed himself.

Iris unscrewed the lights to where they would flicker on and off. Playing into his captive's fears. He slowly reached for his mask and pulled it over his face. Walking eerily towards his next victim.

The pillowcase was ripped off his head abruptly. As the man in the chair screamed in horror from the flashes of light and dark, a demonic figure sauntered towards him with a misshapen face. No mouth. No nose. No form. Just a sadistic emptiness.

A white face with a single twisted blood red eye lit up amongst the darkness.

An image of horror for this man in his last few moments.

"Where is Alfred Mason?" Iris asked.

The man told Iris everything he needed to know. Begging for freedom from this nightmare. He tried to bargain for his life, but there was no use. The drugs had done their damage.

Iris grabbed the man's skull then pressed his thumbs into the man's eyes. Blood and viscera caked Iris's fingers.

Screams echoed throughout the house until it finally fell silent.

Walking out of the room the doorway revealed a lifeless corpse slumped up in a chair. His eyes gone. An eternal expression of crying.

Streams of crimson tears running down his pale face.

CHAPTER 29-

Iris emerged from the room of horrors. Wiping blood and brain matter from his thumbs. Red stood there in shock. Wondering what had happened to the young man he used to know.

"What the fuck happened in there Iris?" Red asked

"Only what was necessary" Iris replied with a dark soulless tone in his voice.

Red silently wept inside for his old friend. He could see the light inside Iris was gone. He could not recognize the man in front of him anymore.

The girl ran up to Iris hugging him and sobbing. He consoled her and led her downstairs.

Red made his way downstairs to see his butler lifeless in a pool of blood. Kneeling he said his goodbyes.

"goodbye old chap, may you rest easy forever" Red spoke softly as a tear rolled down his face.

Walking around to check the bodies of his victims he came across Coopers lifeless corpse. He patted around his armor until he found a phone.

Grabbing the phone, he flipped the body over and spit on it.

"Good riddance" Iris said aloud.

Inside James struggled with what he was seeing. Cooper had betrayed him, but he was the only friend he ever had.

He was like a little brother to him at their best. At their worst they were sworn enemies. Yet he still never expected to be in this position.

"Lets get going" James told Iris.

Making their way downstairs to talk to Red they saw all the damage they had brought to this innocents man's home. Guilt swept over both Iris and James.

"We never should have come here Iris" James spoke inward.

"I know. I fucked up. I got that man killed over there" Iris replied to his soul locked companion.

Iris walked up to Red and gave him a hug. He explained he had to leave before he brought anymore danger to his friend. They agreed Red would take the girl and hide at one of his homes in Europe.

"I'll contact you when you two are safe again" Iris told Red.

"How will you do that?" The girl asked.

Iris looked out past the bullet ridden mosaic glass. Staring off. He turned to them and replied.

"By killing every last one of them."

He walked out of the once pristine and historic home. Now it laid in shambles. Sounds of police sirens wailing in the distance grew closer.

Walking away from the carnage James spotted coopers old truck. They got inside and found the keys in the ignition. Engine roaring, they sped away.

Iris looked down at the phone he grabbed from Coopers corpse. Scrolling through he found the contact he wanted. He dialed the number and waited. The rings went on for a moment before a voice spoke.

"Is the job done?" Alfred Mason spoke from the other end.

Iris stayed silent for a moment. Letting the tension linger.

"Cooper is dead Alfred; I'm coming for you. It does not matter how long it takes. How many of your men I must kill. I will get to you. That's a promise" Iris replied.

Tossing the phone over a nearby bridge he drove into the distance. Wondering what their next move would be.

On the other end of the call Alfred had an expression of anger and terror.

He hung up the phone and called another number.

"Agent cooper is dead. Extract the bodies. Burn the house. Start up project titan. Its time" Alfred hung up the phone. He smashed his hands down on his desk.

"It seems you are not as capable as we once thought Mr. Mason" A shadowed figure spoke from across Alfred's office.

Making his way into the light a man with devilish eyes and gray hair approached. He wore a dark navy-blue suit and had sigils tattooed all over his hands.

"I will fix this" Alfred replied nervously.

"This is your last chance, or we will take what is owed" The mysterious man replied.

He walked across the room and put a hand on Alfred's shoulder.

"The time of the false god is over my pupil. The old ones will rise again."

"Yes, lord Ares" Alfred said as he kneeled to his mentor.

Chapter 30-

Iris drove for hours. Heading north for the Canadian wilderness. Somewhere to lay low and sort things out. He had dealt a significant blow to the Harvester Network, but at a terrible cost. In the small amount of time that he joined this fight he saw countless innocent killed.

Most of them directly because of his own actions.

James struggled internally as well. He had finally gotten the revenge he begged for, but it did not feel right. Cooper was just a pawn in the bigger game. The next move had to attack the hierarchy directly.

It needed to shake the very foundation the Harvester Network worked so hard to build. An attack that would scare them into hiding but would open a small window to clean house.

"What is next?" Iris asked.

The sun started to set behind the old truck. Darkness hitting the bloodied bandages and bags of guns in the back seat.

"Now we wait and plan" James replied.

As they began to exit for the highway a car parked close by began to follow. It mimicked their every turn and held their speed.

James and Iris were too tired to notice their tail.

In the pursuing vehicle a phone begins to ring.

"Target in sight, following now" A man with an Irish accent spoke into the phone.

"Keep tabs on them. No matter how long it takes. Keep them safe" A Russian woman's voice says sternly.

Natasha sets down her phone and lets out a loud sigh.

"Do not worry my child, the light always prevails" A comforting but stern voice spoke from the darkness of the room Natasha was in.

Stepping forward was a beautiful woman. She looked older but full of youth at the same time.

"I've lost strength mother Gaia." Natasha said softly as she let out a tear.

Gaia wiped the tear from Natasha's eye then walked over to a dying plant in the window seal. She dropped the tear drop onto the withered flower.

In moments, the stock grew strong and green. The petals bloomed with vibrant colors.

That sight of wonder made Natasha smile a little bit.

"My dear child save all your strength for the battles ahead." Gaia spoke reassuringly.

A loud cough broke their conversation. A tall skeletal man walked over. The smell of flowers and death followed.

Standing in between Natasha and Gaia the skeleton rested a hand on both of their shoulders.

"The war has just begun" Charon spoke.

END OF BOOK ONE.

Made in the USA
Columbia, SC
09 August 2021